THE CHAMPAGNE BANDITS

The Champagne Bandits gleefully chalk up another substantial untaxed contribution to their assets. But they hear of a bizarre mischance which has put one of their operatives in the power of the police, and could reveal the conspirators' identity to Scotland Yard's Robbery Squad. Immediately, desperate measures are taken to remove the evidence. But swift improvisations, however brilliant, are open to mischance and miscalculation.

P. A. FOXALL

THE CHAMPAGNE BANDITS

Complete and Unabridged

LINFORD
Leicester

First published in Great Britain in 1983 by
Robert Hale Limited
London

First Linford Edition
published 1998
by arrangement with
Robert Hale Limited
London

British Library CIP Data

Foxall, P. A. (Peter Augustus), *1923 –*
    The champagne bandits.—Large print ed.—
Linford mystery library
    1. Detective and mystery stories
    2. Large type books
    I. Title
    823.9'14 [F]

ISBN 0–7089–5349–2

Published by
F. A. Thorpe (Publishing) Ltd.
Anstey, Leicestershire

Set by Words & Graphics Ltd.
Anstey, Leicestershire
Printed and bound in Great Britain by
T. J. International Ltd., Padstow, Cornwall

This book is printed on acid-free paper

1

It was on September 3rd — anniversary of another famous committal to war — an afternoon heavy and somnolent in the summer heat, down a leafy residential avenue in Dulwich, where the most violent thing that ever happened was a dog peeing up a lamp-post, that the bandits struck. Their target was a fat security van delivering two hundred thousand pounds of crisp, freshly printed bank-notes to a South London branch bank. Their technique was ruthless, meticulously rehearsed, co-ordinated like a military operation.

A nondescript lorry shot out of a side road into the avenue and stopped right in the path of the sedate, unsuspecting prize, forcing it to an undignified halt. Simultaneously a pick-up truck that had suddenly loomed up behind screeched to a halt alongside the target vehicle. A fearsome crew of well tooled-up hoodlums dressed in army combat gear, their faces hidden by stocking masks, erupted from the assault vehicles and charged to the attack.

While three of them smashed the side windows and windscreen of the security van and squirted jets of ammonia into the faces of the guards, two more men started up a motorised chain-saw apiece and attacked the rear doors of the prize. Amid showers of sparks and the screech of hardened saw teeth on softer metal, they opened up the high-value van like a can of beans in a matter of seconds.

Even as the startled residents of middle-class Dulwich gathered at their front doors and windows and on their well tailored lawns in shocked, disbelieving horror at the spectacle, the bandits were transferring four green boxes, packed respectively with twenty-, ten-, five- and one-pound notes from the ravished security van to their own pick-up truck. Then they threw in their chain-saws and ammonia sprays and all piled in after it. The souped-up truck roared away like a sports car from the scene of the crime, leaving the attack lorry stuck across the road at right-angles to the traffic to cause the maximum confusion. The whole operation was over in little more than a minute.

By the time the police arrived, the five bandits had switched vehicles at a pre-arranged venue two miles away. In a deserted side street of boarded-up houses awaiting demolition and redevelopment, they quickly tore off their combat jackets and army denim trousers, revealing respectable city suits underneath. They transferred the chain-saws, their weapons, the loot and themselves to two large estate cars. Then they drove off in different directions to an agreed rendezvous.

They were all cold, brutal professionals who'd been on similar set-piece, well rehearsed gravy-runs before, and they knew the drill exactly. The newly printed bank money with its serial numbers on record would have to be laundered before they dared go out and spend it. But they were quite happy to leave this technicality to the operation's organisers, and wait for a week or two before they received their agreed cut in safe, anonymous, well thumbed paper money.

The two men who controlled and directed them were both men of substance whom detectives of Scotland Yard's Robbery Squad described as Champagne Bandits, acting out of greed rather than need. Their exploits followed a disturbing trend in the development of modern organised crime and the execution of dangerous, violent robberies which too often went undetected. These men had fallen foul of the imbecile law years ago and in their inimical contempt for its lumbering, blundering asininity they were bent on flouting it in every way they could, naturally with an eye to maximum profits.

Victor Mannion the senior partner was in his fifties, a big hulking bear of a man, thick-set and muscle-bound like an all-in wrestler, who'd started life as a stunt-man in a travelling circus. He'd begun to make his fortune very early on by flogging everything that wasn't nailed down. Then he'd branched out into

4

business and in his case the hair-line gap between entrepreneurial enterprise and outright villainy was very quickly crossed. He'd had his collar felt of course by hovering lawmen, but they'd never done him any serious harm and certainly had never checked his steady accumulation of wealth over the years.

So now Vic Mannion lived in a grand Regency-style house worth a quarter of a million on Hampstead Heath, indulging himself with lovely girls, night clubs, race-horses and all the other degenerating luxuries that belonged to his station in life. But he would soon have lost his self-respect if he'd lived exclusively for pleasure like the other flabby old drones in his age and status group, so he retained a creative and constructive interest, fortified by lucrative bonuses, by being a working villain. Naturally he was always the Top Brass who did the brain work and never soiled his hands with the unpleasantness of actually stealing money on the highway. He kept his ear well tuned to the criminal grape-vine and when he knew of a soft lucrative target craving to be hit, he tooled up and hit it.

Even in his expensive suits Vic Mannion looked the part of a self-made villain. His square jaw was stuffed with gold fillings. His heavy head was thrust aggressively forward, with coarse reddish hair, a grossly fleshed face and close-set greenish eyes that regarded everybody with a steely, speculative glow.

His partner, Joseph James Blackstock, was several years younger than Vic, still in his early forties, and he too was wealthy enough to regard crime as a stimulating diversion, a challenge to his manhood and a never-failing source of excitement. Unlike Mannion he'd been born rich, his father being a successful money-broker in the City. But with the life of a drone and a playboy practically inflicted on him against his will, and having no virtuous vocation in which to channel his energies, Joe Blackstock was driven by a dissatisfied, burning restlessness to achieve something on his own against all the odds. Criminal enterprise was like a drug to him.

It gave the satisfying thrill of an adventurous world he could recreate in no other way.

Apart from this shared amoral hostility to Society, he looked a most unlikely partner for Mannion, which was why C11 [Criminal Intelligence], the department of Scotland Yard which maintains observation of and documentation on the activities of known and suspected criminals, had so far failed to spot the liaison between them. Joe was suave and charming with the ex-public schoolboy's veneer of civilised living. He was tall, agile, slender as a whip, a dark flashing man with hard eyes and a soft smile. He was sharp as a blade and darkly handsome with a raffish pointed beard over his muscular throat. Whether the rip-off involved the smooth wiles of the con man or the brutal physical activity of the heavy villain, Joe Blackstock was equally at home and equally formidable. The only man who'd ever betrayed him was dead.

He and Mannion respected each other for their toughness, cunning, business

7

ability and lack of scruple. They'd been partners for some years now, co-operating in numerous shady ventures to their mutual profit. Each one knew that to double-cross his partner would mean a sticky end for one or the other or both. It was a good pragmatic working arrangement.

Joe Blackstock was known to the police and had a few minor convictions for handling drugs and smuggling gold. But though they suspected his more serious criminal activities, they'd never been able to put together enough evidence to build a case against him. He had in fact been one of the five-man team which hit the bank security van in Dulwich. He'd led and supervised the whole operation, attending to such vital details as ensuring that all the team wore surgical gloves on the job, double-checking that all the vehicles used were roadworthy and in the right position at the right time, disposing afterwards of the chain-saws, combat gear and other accessories which might give the enemy a clue. In the attack Joe had driven the pick-up truck, smashed the windscreen of the security van and immobilised the driver with an ammonia spray. He had also taken charge of all the stolen money afterwards, when the assault team split up.

2

At quarter to four that afternoon Victor Mannion, relaxing beside his swimming-pool and enjoying the best view in the world over Hampstead Heath towards the mistshrouded city to the south, received the expected phone call from his partner in the field. He picked up the receiver on its long extension cable from the house, and heard Joe Blackstock's guarded voice.

'Mr Mannion?'

'Speaking.'

'This is your money broker. The shares you ordered have been credited to your portfolio.'

'Good. Fine,' grunted Vic with a wolfish grin of triumph. 'No problems then?'

'None at all. We got them at the right price.'

'Right. I'll be in touch,' said Vic, laughing aloud as he put down the telephone.

It always tickled him pink the way Joe gave him news over the phone in bureaucratic gobbledegook when he was reporting the outcome of a job, just as if he expected all the flapping ears of Scotland Yard to be permanently plugged in to Vic's phone. Neither of them suspected as yet that the Dulwich robbery was going to be brutally different from the sequence of successes hitherto.

Feeling the surge of adrenalin that always hit him after the achievement of another victory, that was going to swell his bank balance with yet another five-figure sum, Vic Mannion became distinctly horny in the summer heat and went prowling in search of Erika Fontaine, his current living-in friend who'd gone indoors to take a shower. After rubbing her delicate Scandinavian skin with suntan lotion all afternoon Erika was in dire need of hot water and scented foam.

She was a buxom blonde night-club artiste, stagenamed Miss Midnight, a high-powered sex bomb always on the point of detonation. She had a forty-inch bust, a generous disposition and a mind like a calculator. The way she did her pelvic work-out in the dance, with her languidly flaunting ostrich plumes just permitting the barest glimpse of a blonde pubic hair or two was enough to send any man's blood pressure right off the clock.

Vic had felt his libido swelling to bursting-point as he watched her gyrations. He knew he had to have her, no matter what she cost him. So he invited her to a champagne supper at the Savoy and made her an offer. She'd moved into the Hampstead mansion several months ago, making the whole place seethe and crackle with sexually charged tension, goading Vick to a frenzy with her flashing eyes and teasing laughter. She was costing him an awful lot of money, and, what was much worse, she was getting under his skin with the gnawing unease of sexual jealousy. He was a violently possessive man with his women as with his money, and he knew deep down that Erika was an amoral alley cat. She'd put out for anything in trousers that caught her passing fancy or offered to pay her inflated price. Vic was torturing himself by imagining what she might be up to when she went off into town in the little car he'd given her, having assured him in honeyed tones that she was merely off on a shopping spree. God help her and the miserable gigolo concerned if Vic ever found her two-timing him.

That fateful evening when the hot sun was declining over the Heath, and Vic, full of good food and wine, with his sexual appetite exhaustively assuaged by Erika's incomparable bag of tricks, was just clipping the end off a post-prandial six-inch cigar to inhale with his old French brandy, the telephone rang shrilly like a harbinger of doom.

It was Vic's solicitor, Reuben Levine of Chancery Lane, criminal lawyer extraordinary, who worked round the clock to circumvent the course of Justice and to keep his big-paying clients like Victor Mannion and Joseph Black-stock from getting their just deserts.

'Victor,' he said tensely. 'Did you know that Tom Garbutt has just been arrested?'

13

'What! When?'

'About an hour ago. His wife rang me asking me to go to Walthamstow Police Station and have him released on bail.'

Vic felt his knees turn to jelly with panic fear, for Tom Garbutt was one of the heavies who'd hit the bank security van that afternoon.

'Well?' he blustered. 'And did you spring him?'

'No. The superintendent wouldn't hear of it. He said a serious crime had been committed. Garbutt is helping with enquiries, and further investigations have yet to be made.'

'Did you get a chance to talk to Garbutt?'

'Of course. He's a very frightened man. He says the police are trying to stitch him up on a murder charge that he had nothing to do with.'

Vic exhaled noisily down the phone with relief at the realisation that Garbutt's arrest at this time was pure coincidence. It was the local Divisional Police, not Scotland Yard's Robbery Squad, that had arrested Garbutt, so it could have nothing to do with the operation he'd taken part in that afternoon. And Garbutt was a hard case who'd done time before and would never grass as long as his missis was looked after while he was away, and he had a nice nest-egg to come back to. He was as safe as a rock.

'So why are you bothering me, Rube, with some other loser's bad luck?' said Vic genially. 'You know Tom Garbutt means nothing to me, and if he gets in any trouble he's old enough to get out of it himself, or pay the score.'

'I can't go into details over the phone, Victor,' said Levine ominously. 'I'm on my way over to see you now. Give me twenty minutes.'

An hour later, after Reuben Levine's metallic bronze Rolls Royce Silver Ghost had purred away, Vic Mannion was grey-faced, his eyes glazed with shock, shattered and close to panic at the news his lawyer had brought. Already Vic was out of his depth and needed the wordly sophistication of Joe Blackstock to show him a way out.

He immediately rang Joe's luxury flat

in Belgravia and fortunately Joe was at home. After a heavy and fruitful day he was relaxing in staid domesticity with a case of champagne, an exotic Italian meal sent in from a nearby restaurant and a dolly-bird hostess from one of the numerous clubs he belonged to. He was just getting down to it with her and wasn't very pleased when he heard the anxious voice of an extremely rattled Vic Mannion clamouring for an instant meeting.

'Oh, for Christ's sake, Vic! Can't it wait till the morning?'

'No, it bloody well can't. I've just had Rube Levine here. Even though he is a bloody old woman who takes his umbrella under the shower, he's right this time. It's a real danger we're facing, something really bent. You could have your collar felt by the morning if you don't move fast.'

Joe started to feel equally rattled but was too smooth to show it.

'OK,' he said curtly. 'The usual place. Be there in twenty minutes.'

The usual place was the private room

at the back of a Soho night club called Boobs, in which Mannion was a sleeping partner with a controlling interest. Whenever they met, each man arrived separately and left at a different time in order not to alert any prowling nark from C11 that Mannion and Blackstock were in business together, cooking up some stroke against the Queen's Peace, her Crown and Dignity.

When the obsequious club manager had brought them a silver tray with a bottle of Scotch, a soda syphon and a silver bowl containing ice cubes, and they were alone in the unbugged room, Joe Blackstock said: 'What the hell's got to you, Vic? You look just about ready to climb up the wall. I must say it's not your style to hit the panic button this time of night when we're all standing down and relaxed.'

'Relaxed my arse! We'll do a lot of relaxing in the Scrubs! How far would you trust Tom Garbutt?'

'Garbutt? As far as I'd trust any other mechanic I've ever worked with. He's hard all right, a good reliable worker,

17

cool under pressure. He pulls a real mean stroke with a chain-saw, and was a star performer at this afternoon's caper. He's crazy about big-money pay-offs.'

'That's not what I mean. Would you trust him not to grass if the fuzz put him under real pressure?'

'I can't set your mind at rest there, Vic. You know as well as I do, everybody's got his price and his breaking-point. Why? What's suddenly got you so worried about Tom Garbutt?'

Vic told him succinctly what he'd just heard from Reuben Levine.

'The stupid bastard's got himself arrested on a murder rap, and he's bang to rights. He'll come up for trial and they'll put him away. With his G.B.H. and armed-robbery record and all his other form, he'll probably go down for thirty years, with the Judge urging discretion about parole.'

'How come he's bang to rights?' said Joe aghast. 'Has the bloody fool confessed?'

'There was a snot-nosed little nark called Fred Hider, a private investigator who works over in Garbutt's home patch in Walthamstow. He was found dead last night, strangled with wire in his car in a side street. One of Garbutt's palm prints was found low down on the back of the back seat where he'd crouched, waiting for Hider to come back from some shifty narking job. Garbutt wiped off all his other prints but forgot about the back of the seat he'd touched. He's got no alibi for the time of the murder, and he'd got a two-hundred-per-cent motive for topping Hider.'

'Christ!' swore Joe. 'How was that then?'

'Garbutt was screwing some expensive broad who likes rough trade, the young wife of a Walthamstow pub owner. This middle-aged loser is jealous as hell, with good reason. He suspected she was getting it elsewhere, so he hired Hider the private eye to keep tabs on Garbutt and catch him at it. Hider was watching Garbutt round the clock, and was right behind him when Garbutt broke into a bonded warehouse in Greenwich and got away with a truck-load of French brandy.

19

Thinking he'd broken into the big time with something really heavy on Garbutt, and being a natural-born blackmailer, this miserable little shit Fred Hider is daft enough to go to Garbutt and try to shake him down for a piece of the action. 'Divi up half the take for that brandy heist,' he said, 'or I'll deliver my report on what happened at the Greenwich warehouse to the fuzz.' '

'A certain fast ticket to the boneyard trying to put the black on Tom Garbutt,' commented Joe. 'How did the fuzz get on to all this?'

'Fred Hider the nark had left a full report on it in his personal diary at home. His wife turned it over to the fuzz when Hider turned up dead. Garbutt never bargained for that.'

'My God, what a stinking mess,' groaned Joe. 'I can guess what's coming. Garbutt's going to do a deal, isn't he?'

Vic nodded sombrely.

'Too bloody right he is. According to Rube Levine, the Robbery Squad have already moved in on him. Flaps Pritchard — him with the elephant's ears — is dangling a thirty-year stretch for murder under Garbutt's nose, with an option of a clean sheet and a new identity if he'll turn Supergrass on all his other activities, and name the men he's worked for. Flaps Pritchard knows bloody well that Garbutt's been in on half the blagging jobs done in the past couple of years, and can finger everybody who was in with him. That includes you, Joe. And then they'll be turning over stones to find the link between you and me. They'll never bloody rest till they've stitched us up and put us away. We can't just hope that Garbutt will refuse the offer and go down like a bloody hero to do his thirty years. What would you do if you were in Garbutt's shoes and saw a chance of ducking a real life sentence?'

'I'd grass,' said Joe promptly. 'I'd shop the bloody Pope himself for that kind of a deal.'

'So what are we going to do?'

'Obvious,' retorted Joe savagely. 'Garbutt will have to go.'

'How?'

'Get to him while he's still in the local

nick at Walthamstow. I know it'll cost a fortune, and it'll have to be done fast before he agrees to take the bait. Once he's started spilling the beans they'll put maximum protection on him and move him around from one nick to another so that we'll never get to him. It's got to be tonight, Vic.'

'What if he's already started, and grassed about this afternoon's job?' said Vic with deep pessimism. 'The fuzz could already be out looking for you with a warrant. The take will be too hot even to launder for a good many months. It might be safer to dump it now, destroy the evidence altogether. Without that for a clincher, even Supergrass testimony would be iffy. Where is the take, by the way?'

'Locked in the boot of my car, parked just round the corner.'

'Christ!' muttered Vic. 'Is that wise? Your car is the first thing they'll turn over as soon as they hear a whisper about you. Cut your losses, Joe. Dump it in the river, tonight, now. There'll always be other heists, but not if you're banged

22

up in the Scrubs. Why take chances when you don't have to?'

'Here, hang on a bit,' protested Joe. 'Two hundred grand is a bit too tasty to run out on in a panic. I really sweated for it this afternoon, put fifteen years of my life on the line, and what I've won I hang on to. That's the streak of Abraham's blood in me, for which I have no foreskin. We don't know for sure yet that Garbutt's grassed about this afternoon. The chances are I've still got time to move about. So if I can't launder the new notes over here, why don't I take it in a suitcase to Switzerland, change it into francs at 3.79 to the pound and deposit it in my numbered account? The Gnomes of Zurich don't ask embarrassing questions about the serial numbers of foreign currency notes as long as it's all legal tender. The Swiss franc is a good hard currency that never depreciates.'

Vic Mannion took a vigorous swallow at his whisky, rattling the ice cubes against his dentures, and frowned dubiously.

'A whole suitcase full of folding

23

money?' he queried. 'How the hell are you going to pull that off? The fuzz will be expecting freshly printed money to go abroad. After today's heist in Dulwich they'll have all the airports sewn up, on the look-out for somebody like you.'

'I wouldn't attempt to get it through customs and embarkation in the usual way,' replied Joe. 'I'll wangle an unofficial lift with Rollo Seaton on one of his tourist charter flights from Gatwick first thing in the morning. He's brought in cannabis and scag, and taken out gold for us, at a price. So he'll manage to fit me aboard with the tourists for a quick hop to Basle, and no questions asked.'

'Yes, that's not a bad idea,' conceded Vic in a relieved tone. 'Good thinking, Joe. A bent airline pilot is the answer to everybody's prayer, as long as he hasn't got a clue what you're transporting in your bulky suitcase. Seaton is a flash bugger, too ready to go bent for nothing. I wouldn't trust him an inch.'

'Would I be likely to make a general public announcement that I'm exporting a hijacked bank-roll?' said Joe ironically.

'If it'll put your mind at rest, I'll go straight from here to Seaton's pad in Raynes Park and get it all fixed up for tomorrow. Then even if the fuzz do want my help with their enquiries, I'll be in Switzerland while they're looking in all my usual haunts.'

The partners went on to discuss other aspects of urgent fence-mending in the current dangerous crisis that was upon them. The priority measure was getting a reliable assassin into the Walthamstow Police Station to silence Tom Garbutt in his cell before he could accept Scotland Yard's tempting offer to become a Supergrass. By spreading enough four-figure sums around, Vic Mannion thought he saw an even chance of bringing it off before morning, while Joe was sure he could pull the proceeds of their latest bank-robbery success out of the fire.

On this note of guarded optimism the two partners went their different ways.

3

Rowland Cuthbert Seaton was a Senior Captain for the air charter company Air Mercury, based at Gatwick and flying BAC 1-11 jets on the short-haul tourist shuttle to Europe. Rowland, or Rollo, as he preferred to be called, was in his middle forties now, dashing, raffish and debonair, with dark wavy hair going grey at the temples in the most distinguished way. His elegant wisp of a moustache and his charismatic air of swinging depravity made him look a bit like Errol Flynn, that classic, old-hat Hollywood swashbuckler. So being justly proud of his heaven-sent resemblance to the saint and hero of middle-aged, sex-crazed roués, Rollo went out of his way to cultivate the role.

He made it a point of honour to lay every hostess who served aboard his aircraft. If she was new and virtuous he would have her no later than the second trip out. It was his proud boast that he wouldn't have a filly working aboard his aircraft who wouldn't heave to for her captain. This was despite the fact that he was very much married, with an imposing heavily mortgaged house in the best residential area of Raynes Park, a family of three young children, and a good-looking young wife with some money of her own who hadn't yet given up trying to turn Rowland into a decent, hard-working, law-abiding mouse.

Rollo Seaton had first met Joe Blackstock when they were both young, carefree, footloose adventurers, looking for kicks and easy money and working as mercenary pilots for beat-up Dakotas in Tshombe's ramshackle air force in the Congo débâcle of the early sixties. Being equally bent, opportunistic and pleasure-loving, the two men had hit it off well together and had kept in touch afterwards to their mutual profit. Seaton, the small-town son of a local government official had always secretly envied Blackstock the money-broker's son, born to the purple of commerce. So whenever he engaged in some shady operation with his old buddy, Seaton always bargained hard to make a handsome profit. Nothing would have pleased him better than the life of a wealthy drone, but he'd had to earn his living by flying aircraft in various parts of the world. He'd been kicked out of the United States under a cloud while working on one of their small domestic airlines, for a big haul of heroin had been found aboard his aircraft when he flew it back to Washington from New Mexico.

Afterwards he'd lived a haphazard, buccaneering life, smuggling illicit diamonds into Amsterdam, flying out raw opium from Burma or pure heroin from Hong Kong. He was an indefatigable pioneer who measured the risk factor solely in terms of financial profit. Even now, in outwardly respectable middle age, with a responsible job, twenty-eight thousand pounds a year and a stake in Society as householder, husband and parent, Rowland Seaton was still up to his tricks, for to him life without a fast buck was insupportable. He was always ready to smuggle a high-value package in or out of the country aboard his aircraft. The Mannion/Blackstock consortium put plenty of such business his way and paid him a handsome fee. But it was such an easy milk run with no great fortune involved that Seaton regarded it as going straight. His swashbuckling heart was always hankering after bending the rules in more spectacular style and making a far bigger tax-free percentage.

He had a feeling deep in his bones that something like this was about to happen when his doorbell rang at eleven o'clock on the night of September 3rd and Joe Blackstock stood in the portico looking cool and immaculate and well groomed as ever. It was quite without precedent for Joe to seek him out on his own home ground late at night. A leisurely arrangement by telephone was the usual way they met to do business when Joe needed some smuggling done. So Rollo's shrewd cunning promptly worked it out that Joe's unexpected visit meant he must be in a bit of a bind.

'Come on in, Joe,' he said affably, standing aside in the doorway. 'Phyllis has just gone up to bed, and I'm in attendance for a command performance when I've locked up and put the mutt to bed, so you can't stay long.'

'I don't need to,' said Joe as he walked into the tastefully decorated entrance hall.

'So what's the proposition this time?'

'I just wanted to know if you're still on the morning milk run to Basle with the package trippers.'

'Sure. Loading at nine a.m. with a complement of a hundred and four passengers plus baggage. Ready to roll at nine-thirty. Unless there's some hold-up getting clearance from the Tower, we shall be airborne before ten o'clock.'

'That'll do fine,' said Joe. 'Any chance of giving me a lift to Basle, Rollo? You know the form. Make out I'm a crew member and get me aboard without going through the customs shed.'

Seaton turned down the corners of his handsome mouth with wary and disapproving reluctance.

'I don't know about that, Joe. You're asking me a hell of a lot. Company rules are very strict about carrying unauthorised passengers, and they've been tightened up a lot recently. It's my job on the line if there should be a spot check by a company inspector. With airlines as big as Laker going bust, what chance is there for me to get another job if I get fired by Air Mercury for improper conduct?'

'Oh, come on, Rollo. Don't be a wet nellie. Has marriage softened your brain up or something? You know I always pay well, cash on the nail.'

'Yes, but this is a bit different from the odd kilo of scag or a little bag of ice, isn't it? If you just tagged along with the trippers I could disown you when you were sussed. But taking you aboard under my own personal escort, Jesus wept! Why can't you go through the customs sheds anyway, or go on your own passport on a scheduled flight if it comes to that? Are you hot with the law, by any chance?'

'Of course not,' said Joe hastily. 'I've just got an urgent appointment in Basle tomorrow morning, and at this short notice you're the most reliable means of getting me there.'

'Oh yes? And what will you have tucked into your hand-baggage that you don't want the customs narks to get a look at?'

'Nothing,' said Joe, spreading his hands in a gesture of disarming candour. 'Look here, it's worth five hundred quid to me to get aboard your plane in the morning. You can have the cash in advance right now.'

He promptly produced his cheque-book and a gold Parker pen and started to write.

'Not enough,' said Seaton, his dissolute face hardening with obdurate greed. 'For the risk I'll be running it's just bloody beer money, and you know it.'

'All right. I can go to a grand then.'

'Make it two grand, and in addition I'll need to sweeten the rest of the crew, because they'll know you're not legit. If they're on the take as well they won't shop me, will they? So add on another grand to split among them.'

Joe hesitated, screwed up his mouth with extreme reluctance and distaste and finally nodded in agreement.

'OK then, you bloody extortioner. I'll be looking round for another courier in future.'

He started to write out the cheque.

'Hold your horses,' said Rollo with a twisted grin. 'I want genuine folding money, not cheques. It's not that I think your cheque is likely to bounce, Joe. But Phyl and I have got a joint bank account now — her idea, not mine — and if she sees an extra three grand going in suddenly, she'll keep on nagging at me to tell her where it came from and prove it's not bent. To tell you the truth I've run out of ideas to convince her, and she's so bloody persistent. So anything I get on the side from now on has got to be spot cash. No cash, no deal.'

Joe hesitated in a quandary. He had the two hundred grand from the day's robbery locked in the boot of his car, so giving Rollo his three grand on the nail was not a logistical problem. The risk lay in Seaton's splashing it about in the usual reckless fashion on broads, booze and gambling when it was hot virginal money in series with all the serial numbers publicised as stolen. However, that was a far more remote risk than the one Joe would face if he didn't get on that plane first thing in the morning and fly the bulk of the money out of the country. The spice of life lay in balancing one risk against another, making the correct decision to stay ahead of the enemy.

'OK, Rollo, just as you like,' he said lightly. 'I think I can just about raise three grand in folding money. Hang on a sec.'

He went outside to his car, unlocked the boot and opened up one of the green bank boxes containing tenpound notes. The new high-denomination notes were banded in thousands, the singles in packets of a hundred each. Joe took three bundles of tens and took them into the house.

'Lovely!' breathed Rollo, his blase eyes opening a quarter of an inch wider, his lips almost drooling at the sight of it. 'Smell that printing ink! Never been touched by human hand, by the look of it. Here, have you just robbed a bloody bank, you old so-and-so?'

'Now would I do a thing like that?' grinned Joe. 'It's just payment for some merchandise, and the customer distrusts banks and cheques much the same as you do.'

'Fair enough,' said Rollo. 'I'll bank it in my old tool-chest at the back of the garage where Phyl never looks. And I'll see you at ten to nine in the morning outside the staff canteen at Gatwick. Don't be late. I can't get on the blower to the Tower and ask them to delay take-off while my stowaway gets aboard.'

After Joe had driven away Rollo carefully hid his money in the tool-chest under a dusty old work bench in the garage, locked up and went to bed. But his command performance was nowhere near his usual standard that night, for his mind was not on it. He was preoccupied by fascinated thoughts of the ease with which Joe Blackstock had just produced three thousand quid in new-minted money from the boot of his car like a rabbit from a hat, just as if he always carried that amount of ready cash around with him for day-to-day expenses.

He must be on to something really hot, like a licence to print the stuff.

In the end Rollo's frustrated wife flounced away in a huff and turned her back on him for the rest of the night. But Rollo hardly noticed her as he fantasised about inexhaustible supplies of crisp, crinkly ten-pound notes.

4

Unable to go home that night just in case the Robbery Squad was waiting on his doorstep, armed with Tom Garbutt's incriminating information, Joe drove to the Chelsea flat of a casual friend, Lynette Doyle, a Soho exotic dancer who was always happy to turn a trick for Joe as long as she wasn't otherwise engaged. She gave him drinks, a TV dinner, a good balling and bed for the night. Before he left in the morning he borrowed her travelling suitcase, which was new and expensive and made of soft white leather. He wrote her a cheque for two hundred pounds to cover the suitcase and the night in bed. Lynette, as usual delighted by his style, asked him to call again.

On his way to Gatwick Airport with plenty of time in hand, Joe pulled off the road into a quiet wood and started transferring the money from the bank boxes into Lynette's travelling case.

He managed to pack in all the high denominational notes, the twenties, tens and fives, but there wasn't enough room for all the bundles of one-pound notes. He would have to leave behind about ten thousand pounds in single notes. As it went against all his principles to jettison good money that he'd schemed and risked so much to get, he stuffed it in the spare-wheel compartment of his Jaguar. He decided to arrange with Vic Mannion to have the car collected from Gatwick Airport and stored in Vic's garage at Hampstead while he was away. Thus the concealed hoard wouldn't be at risk.

When he'd parked the car in the airport car park he went into the terminal building and found a row of telephones, each equipped with a plastic acoustic shield. He dialled Vic's Hampstead number and Vic, who was still in bed, locked firmly on to Miss Midnight, answered with a sleepy irritable growl at being so rudely disturbed.

'Yes? Who is it?'

'Vic. Joe here. I'm eyeballing the big

bird, ready for migration to the great outdoors. Any last-minute reason why I should abort?'

'It's up to you,' replied Vic casually. 'It was your bright idea to export, and we agreed it was best. I don't see any reason for calling it off.'

'Nothing's changed then? Our pet budgie is still in his cage? You've not scragged him yet?'

'Hell, Joe! Give me a chance. Are you expecting a bloody miracle? I've commissioned a good man, but you can't expect him to walk straightaway into a cage to scrag a budgie. It needs some careful planning.'

'Oh, sure!' retorted Joe bitterly. 'And all this time he could be singing his little songs like budgies always do, singing his heart out to a grateful audience.'

'Well, we allowed for that, didn't we, with the contingency plan. That's why you're booked for export, and I know you'll make a damned good job of it.'

With difficulty Joe swallowed his irritation at the mental image of the fat voluptuary complacently taking it

39

easy in bed, twined all round Miss Midnight, secure in the knowledge that Joe was taking all the risks to get rid of the only evidence that could give him trouble. The heart of the matter was that it didn't really bother Vic whether Tom Garbutt sang his head off or not, as long as the incriminating hot bread was safely interred by Joe in a Swiss bank for future enjoyment. The history of the Mannion/Blackstock partnership to date was that Joe took all the risks while Vic did the staff work.

'Vic, do me a favour, will you?' said Joe smoothly. 'I've had to leave my transport where the big bird roosts. Could you send somebody to pick it up, like today, and garage it till I get back? I don't want to find it stripped down to the hubs and body shell, or towed away by a ringer's team to be flogged in Brussels. There's a spare key taped underneath the off-side front wheel arch, and you know my registration number, JB 2.'

'OK, Joe. I'll see to that for you,' said Vic affably. 'Have fun in the great outdoors.'

He replaced the receiver and went back to his fun with Miss Midnight, while Joe at Gatwick hung up with a sardonic grin. If he'd told Vic that the car was worth nearly double its market value because of the overflow money stashed away in the spare-wheel compartment, canny old Vic would never have gone near it in case it was staked out by the fuzz. As it was, he could take his chance with Tom Garbutt turning Supergrass and putting Joe Blackstock in the frame. Equal risk for equal gain was a much better working arrangement.

Joe was in good time to keep his appointment with Rowland Seaton outside the airport canteen. Rollo looked more like a war-winning Errol Flynn swashbuckler than ever in his dashing Senior Captain's uniform with pilot's wings, four gold rings on his sleeves, yards of gold braid and a peaked cap perched on his head at a rakish angle. It was no more than his right that all the romantic, hero-worshipping air hostesses should adore him.

He took a long hard look at Joe's large

new suitcase, but though he was bursting with curiosity to know what was in it, he didn't say anything. His mind went back automatically to the pristine newness of those bundles of bank-notes that Joe had unloaded so casually from the boot of his car. It was a damned good reason for not wanting to go through customs with the other trippers; to drive up under the wings in a jeep with the aircraft's captain and go aboard like a V.I.P.

The baggage was already being loaded into the belly of the aircraft and Rollo casually asked Joe if he wanted to put his suitcase in with it.

'No thanks,' said Joe. 'I don't like the way they crash them around and make a point of knocking all the corners off. I'll keep this one with me, if you don't mind.'

Rollo made no comment, but his hungry thoughts turned with even greedier intensity to those bundles of crisp, virginal bank-notes that he'd glimpsed and handled last night, like a sinner's glimpse of Paradise.

The hundred-plus happy, chirruping

trippers came streaming out in a long crocodile from the Departure Lounge and went up the steps into the aircraft, while Rollo with his second pilot went through the cockpit check list and the twin jets were started up. Just after nine-thirty he received clearance from Flight Control in the Tower. The jets whined more shrilly as Rollo opened them up, and the aircraft began to roll out towards the runway.

A few minutes later they were airborne, climbing steeply into the clear blue summer sky, with the incredibly green landscape of Sussex falling farther and farther away below.

Joe heaved a deep sigh of contentment as he realised he was safely over the first hurdle. The illicit haul was as good as banked in the deep, impregnable, highly secret vaults of the canny Swiss.

As every passenger seat was occupied Joe had to squeeze into the tiny galley in the tail of the aircraft, where the two hostesses prepared the drinks, the duty-free sales and the plastic in-flight snacks for the passengers. It was hot in the galley and the two adjacent jet engines in the tail, less than a yard away through the body shell, made their presence known intrusively.

Joe sat on a collapsible stool wedged against the emergency door, hugging his precious suitcase to him in his lap, and spent the time agreeably in chatting up the two hostesses. They were very pleasant, bedworthy girls in their pretty pale blue hostess uniforms, the short sheath-like skirt tight round their bottoms, the neatly tailored military style tunic buttoned down the front and the funny little half-conical hat with a curly brim and a soupçon of gold braid, which looked like a Yankee officer's headgear in the Union Cavalry at Gettysburg, 1863.

Sally Crowther, aged twenty-five and still single, was the star of the team in looks as well as seniority. She was blonde, sleek, demure, tall with an excellent figure. It was obvious she was head over heels in love with Rollo Seaton, her pilot and hero. Even though she knew he was very much married and devoted to his children, tied down with a mortgage

44

millstone round his neck, she could never give up hope, fooling herself that one day perhaps the unspecified miracle would happen and Rollo would be hers for ever. As a result of this obsession she looked impersonally, without human interest, at all other men, including Joe Blackstock, as if they were pieces of furniture.

The second hostess, Yvonne Belmondo, was the illicit offspring of a French mother and an Irish father. Her formative years had been spent in France, for which she'd always had an emotional affinity, and she'd taken her mother's name. Yvonne was inclined on occasion to be sullen and temperamental, as if she blamed the rest of mankind for her illegitimacy and somewhat deprived, insecure upbringing. In physique she was dumpy and round as a Russian peasant woman and her complexion was still slightly pitted with some skin ailment of her adolescence. But she had a beautiful smile and perfect teeth, a great asset for the job she was in. She could disarm the hostility of the cantankerous old buffers who came on board, allay the

45

anxieties of children and even soothe the querulous fears of women far gone in pregnancy by flashing her beautiful smile. Her eyes were the darkest blue Joe had ever seen and her slightly husky voice with its strong traces of a French accent worked on a man with undertones of a vibrant sexuality.

Yvonne's physical immediacy, from her well sprung, resilient curves to the sultry mystique she could express in the droop of an eyelid soon had Joe Blackstock hooked with healthy lust. His eyes never left her as she brewed the coffee on the tiny electric stove built at eye-level into the galley. She in her turn was attracted by his instant admiration, his dark, almost sinister good looks, and his blasé air of having had more than enough of everything forbidden or expensive in life. She reciprocated his cheerful banter and sexual suggestions.

'Yvonne,' he said, 'why don't you spend the coming week-end with me in Basle? Switzerland is a grand place to be young in, even though it is owned by arthritic financiers. I'll show you around.'

46

'Oo la la! Le weekend anglais!' giggled Yvonne with a provocative squirm of her well sprung chassis. 'You show me more than around, I think. Besides, we gotta take off on the home run with more tourists at 18.30, don't we, Sally? I don't aim to leave Air Mercury with bad faith and screw up my job so I never get another, just to be shown around a dump like Basle. Not even for you, you big ape.'

'Oh, come on, Yvonne. Don't be old-fashioned,' wheedled Joe. 'There are always good jobs around for girls as tasty as you with all your assets. Why let one job rule your life? Be a sport, Yvonne. Remember, now is forever. Tomorrow just comes and goes. I can get you another job if jobs are all you want. You can be my housekeeper, for instance. I pay good union rates in cash and kind, with superannuation facilities.'

'Oo, you are a big ape!' exclaimed Yvonne, throwing up her hands with mock outrage. 'Sally, did you hear Monsieur's proposition?'

'Easily the most unsubtle approach I've

ever heard,' said Sally with a disdainful sniff. 'Do you think he got that spiel from running a massage parlour?'

'He is a big ape,' said Yvonne fondly. 'I like big apes who like me, whether they come from a massage parlour or wherever. But I don't do all they tell me or I soon be in Queer Street.'

Meanwhile up front on the flight deck Rowland Seaton had levelled out at thirty-five thousand feet, set his course for Basle and locked in the automatic pilot. They were cruising at five hundred and fifty miles an hour under a perfect blue sky with an immense floor of sun-kissed clouds three miles below.

The second pilot, Sandy Wootton, took a copy of that morning's *Sun* newspaper from his brief-case and turned automatically to Page 3, where an enormous pair of mammary orbs with huge spiky nipples seemed to leap out and hit him in the eye. But Rowland Seaton, glancing sideways, hardly noticed the morning's delectation, for he'd caught sight of the headline on Page 2 that startled him into instant awareness.

It said:

CHAIN SAW BANDITS NET £200,000

Avidly Rollo leaned over Sandy Wootton and read the opening paragraph.

'Yesterday afternoon in a quiet Dulwich street, five masked bandits stopped a bank security van on its way to a branch bank with a consignment of bank notes. They smashed the windows with iron bars, immobilised the guards by squirting ammonia in their eyes, and cut open the locked doors with chain saws. A bank spokesman confirmed that £200,000 is missing . . . '

'Wow!' muttered Rollo, his thoughts straying immediately to the three thousand pounds in new, untouched notes that Joe had casually taken from the boot of his car last night to pay him for the ride, just as if it was a self-replenishing hoard.

'That has to be where it all came from,' mused Rollo. 'That's why he's so bloody keen to get to Basle under cover, carrying a big white suitcase that no customs man is allowed to stick his conk into it! It must be him and Mannion branching out into other fields. That money's so hot it would burn a hole through any hiding-place in England, so it's got to go in a Swiss bank vault to cool down. Jesus Christ! Out of two hundred grand the miserable sod only wanted to give me five hundred quid for getting all that jackpot to safety! He should have cut me in for a third at least.'

As Rollo's own avarice was second to none, the mean, cheeseparing ingratitude of his so-called friend left Rollo seething with disgruntled envy and resentment, which he hid easily enough behind his usual charming smile and façade of general bonhomie.

He took off his headphones, handed over control of the aircraft to Sandy Wootton and set his peaked, scrambled-egg-covered cap at its usual jaunty angle on his brow. Then he walked aft from the flight deck, conscious of the admiring eyes of all the lady passengers as he sauntered down the aisle between the two banks of seats and shoved his distinguished, dissolute face round the galley door.

'Everything under control then, girls?' he said breezily. 'Is our stowaway behaving himself, I trust?'

'Sure he is,' replied Yvonne, 'Like a greedy little boy let loose in a sweet-shop.'

'I'm under severe provocation,' said Joe. 'With Yvonne's bottom bobbing in my eye all the time, you could say it's a question of behaviourism rather than behaviour.'

'Good show,' grinned Rollo. 'This is what we call a happy ship. We're all well adjusted here, with normal glandular reactions. Joe, why don't you stretch your legs for a bit. Go up forrard and take my seat for a spell while I go in the lav. Sandy might let you take the controls for a spell if you want to keep your hand in. It's a bit different from the old DC3, as you'll soon find out.'

'Thanks, Rollo. That's not a bad idea,' said Joe, standing up in the claustrophobic galley, glad to escape if only for a short time from such close proximity to the engines' incessant roar.

'You could leave your suitcase here,' said Rollo casually as Joe prepared to set

51

off up the aisle, carrying his large suitcase with him.

'No, I'd better take it out of the way,' said Joe hastily. 'There's no damned room in this galley as it is. The girls will only keep falling over it.'

Clutching the heavy suitcase he walked out of the galley, fondling Yvonne's bottom as he went past her and receiving a warm grin of complicity in return. Curious eyes followed him as he strode between the two crowded rows of chattering trippers packed in like sardines. He was wearing an expensively tailored light-weight suit of pale grey, a white silk shirt and calf-skin boots. With his broad-shouldered, slim-waisted figure, bronzed skin, well trimmed black beard and tidy haircut, he looked like an advertisement for a good brand of whisky or an expensive car in some glossy magazine. Nobody would have taken him at face value for a well adjusted, well organised and completely ruthless hoodlum on his way to bank a stolen haul with the collusive Gnomes. He ducked through the door to the flight deck where everything seemed infinitely remote and technically perfect, where there was only a cosy and reassuring murmur from the two frantic engines in the tail.

As soon as Joe had disappeared Rollo turned to the two girls, his manner urgent, conspiratorial and deadly serious.

'Did you see that?' he whispered. 'The way he won't be parted from that bloody suitcase even for five minutes. He won't let it out of his sight. And do you know why? The bastard's got a fortune tucked away in there, stolen money in clean new notes. He and his partner, a bigger crook than he is, knocked off a bank truck in Dulwich yesterday afternoon. The papers are full of it. The hoods got away with two hundred grand, and Joe's off to bank it in Switzerland till the heat's off.'

'I do not believe it,' said Yvonne, her eyes wide as saucers. 'Joe is not the type to — how you say? — knock off a bank truck or anything else.'

'Don't be stupid,' snarled Rollo. 'Every bugger's the type to knock off a bank if he thinks he can get away with it.

53

Some crooks look smoother than others, that's all.'

'But how do you know he has all that money in his suitcase?' breathed Sally. 'How can you know he had anything to do with a bank raid in Dulwich?'

For answer Rollo took from his inside pocket a wad of new ten-pound notes, part of the payment he'd extorted from Joe for the ride to Basle, and waved it under the noses of the startled girls.

'Just bend your peepers on this stuff. Smell it! Fresh printer's ink. If that's not hot money straight off the presses, I'll never touch money again. Joe gave it to me to pay his fare, and he'd got a whole bloody trunkful of the stuff in his car. It must be the proceeds of a bank robbery. How else could he be in possession of so much freshly printed cash? Why else would he want to bolt to Switzerland in such a hurry with a big suitcase that he didn't want to take through the customs shed? Joe Blackstock always was a fly bastard a couple of moves ahead of the law, him and his rough-neck partner, Vic Mannion. They've been at it for years.

Assuming that he split that two hundred grand even with Mannion — give or take a few grand to pay off the troops on the ground — he'll have about a hundred grand in that suitcase that he won't let go of. Doesn't it unsettle your whole metabolism, girls, to be cheek by jowl in this galley with a big-time hoodlum and all that gravy? Doesn't your natural ambition and sense of justice make you want to get your fingers in it, easy money, tax-free, oodles of it, side-tracked from a lousy criminal?'

'No,' replied Sally, looking at him with maternal tenderness and adoration. 'I don't want anything to do with stolen money, and I don't want you to touch it either, Rollo. Personally I couldn't care less about material wealth. It's us I care about. Let that flashy opportunist keep his stolen money — if he has stolen it. It won't do him any good in the long run.'

Rollo looked at his bed-fellow in gloomy irritation. She was starting to sound just like his wife, carping, reformatory, do-gooding, and that was the reverse of having fun. As if a maudlin sentiment like love, a mere emotional spasm, was all that mattered in life!

'Well, I care about money,' he exclaimed hotly, 'because I have to devote my life to earning it while hungry hands snatch it away as soon as I've got it. For one thing it's against the law to export currency notes in that quantity when the pound is under international pressure. You can't expect crooks like Blackstock to be patriotic. So I reckon it's our duty to get it off him and take it back home to spend, don't you? It's not even as if Blackstock needs the money. He's got plenty already, the greedy bastard. He just collects it and hoards it with a collector's mania like some cranks collect stamps and antique snuff-boxes. How would you like to give up work altogether, Sally, and just live? A villa in the Bahamas, or a flat on Millionaires' Row at Rio, or maybe a dude ranch in the San Fernando Valley. Take your pick. The freedom of choice is yours.'

'I wouldn't mind where I was as long as you were there with me,' declared Sally fervently.

Rollo dismissed the mawkish sentiment with an impatient gesture.

'So how are we going to bring it off then, girls?' he went on with brisk efficiency. 'Blackstock is nobody's fool. He's security-minded even when he's asleep, and he can be a rough bastard when he's in a corner, a typical street brawler. So this necessary divorce from his loot will have to be brought about by guile, especially as he's clinging to that suitcase like a limpet. I want you to put your thinking caps on, girls, between now and touch-down.'

'You can count me out of it,' declared Yvonne icily. 'I like that Joe. I don't believe he is a robber, or got bank money in his suitcase. He looks so innocent. I don't want to touch no nest of snakes like this. Besides, I got no time for lousy low-down thieves.'

'Good God!' exclaimed Rollo, his mouth dropping open in mock horror. 'We've got Virtue aboard! Now how the

57

hell did I ever get landed with a bloody thing like Virtue?'

'You don't know for sure he got money in that suitcase,' protested Yvonne sullenly. 'You don't know nothing. You jump to a lot of crazy conclusions because you want to get rich easy. You slit a man's throat for his suitcase, and then find nothing but his clothes in it.'

'Listen,' said Rollo, glancing furtively round the galley door to make sure Joe wasn't on his way back. 'I've known Joe Blackstock for over twenty years now, and he never does anything without a very sound crooked reason, totally committed to the percentage of profit. Every time he comes to me with a little package for export or import, it's a valuable piece of bent merchandise that he doesn't want the customs officers to get a look at.'

'Well, that's his business,' replied Yvonne stubbornly. 'It don't call for him to get mugged by his so-called friends. I want no part of it, you understand?'

'In that case then, Lady Honesty, you can keep your mouth shut, unless you want me to bloody it up for you,' hissed Rollo savagely. 'If you foul things up for us by tipping him off, I'll make damned sure you never fly with this company again, or fly anywhere except in a bloody wheel-chair.'

His eyes blazed with such murderous ferocity that Yvonne flinched and trembled, even though she'd had an arduous training all through childhood at the hands of a drunken, brawling Irish peasant, always handy with his fists and belt-buckle. She knew how frenziedly sadistic Rollo could be from the one and only time she'd let him ball her. It was in a cheap hotel room at Interlaken and halfway through the performance the worried proprietor had come knocking politely on the locked bedroom door to enquire deferentially why Madame was screaming. Did she need any help?

'I thought Joe was supposed to be your friend,' said Yvonne defiantly. 'A fine friend you turn out to be! I would rather have an enemy.'

Rollo curled his lip in a sneer of aristocratic arrogance.

'Friendship is what you can enjoy before a hundred grand takes over,' he scoffed. 'Nobody but a simple moron puts that kind of value on a sentiment. Do you think anyone goes anywhere or works at anything in this world out of sentiment? Don't be so bloody naive.'

He turned to Sally, his trusted retainer. 'If anybody can turn Joe's head and make him careless, you can,' he said kindly. 'Joe was always a pushover for a beautiful girl who made it clear she was struck on him. So string him along with the old bait, but don't overdo it because he can be shrewd. If he invites you, go to his hotel room and be nice to him. I'll be waiting in the wings to snatch the suitcase as soon as you've worn him to a frazzle and worked him into a coma.'

Sally was deeply hurt at the light-hearted generosity with which her hero was prepared to offer her body like some cheap pimp as a mere decoy in a commercial rip-off.

'Is that all you think of me?' she protested plaintively. 'You'd throw me to him like a piece of meat to a dog, just for a bit of money!'

'Correction, darling. Just for a lot of money,' said Rollo cheerfully. 'And a glorious carefree future for both of us.'

Seeing Sally on the verge of tears, and realising somewhat belatedly that you can't afford to treat a woman's emotions light-heartedly when you want something from her, he quickly became tender and conciliatory. He kissed her lovingly and fondled her crotch in a very special way he had that sent her over the moon.

'You know what I mean, Sally. You're a clever girl. You can decoy him easily enough just by being yourself. Keep him talking in the hotel bar, or get him to take you to a restaurant while I just nip up to his hotel room where he's left the suitcase. You don't really have to give him as much as a chaste sisterly kiss unless you want to.'

'I can't stand the man,' said Sally vehemently. 'He's too suave and slick and sure of himself. There's something — I don't know what — almost sinister about him. He obviously thinks he's God's gift to women, and everybody's

61

his for the taking. Besides, if he is a robber and a violent man like you say he is, isn't he likely to turn vicious as soon as he suspects I'm trying to fool him? Oh darling, I'm so frightened. I don't want to be at his mercy when he finds out I helped you to steal his suitcase.'

'Oh, come on. Relax,' pleaded Rollo. 'We'll both be long gone by the time he finds out he's been done. This is not like my Sally, a brave girl like you. I can guarantee he won't get nasty with you. Joe is a real gentleman with women, just straight sex and no rough stuff. I remember when we were in the Congo, living it up a bit in Brazzaville. A little dumb Belgian blonde he was crazy about, the wife of a Belgian Army officer, took Joe to the cleaners for a thousand dollars. And he didn't even bother to go after her and break her back. He just said, *'C'est la guerre!'* or something equally bloody fatuous, and wrote the money off with the tart.'

'But — '

'My guess is he'll check in at a hotel

first. He usually stays at the Montana when he's in Basle. Pretty soon after that he'll start going round the money changers to convert that hot sterling into Swiss francs. He won't dare change the whole lot at one money shop in case they take fright at such a haul, suspect it's hot money and tip off the police or Interpol. He won't be able to bank a whole bloody suitcase in the hotel safe that's probably only big enough for some old girl's diamond ear-rings and pearl necklace. So common sense dictates he'll keep the suitcase with him till he's converted the sterling and banked the proceeds. When he's unloaded a thousand or two, he'll be looking round for a diversion and some light entertainment. That's where you come in on cue to help his relaxation, Sally.'

'I'll do anything for you, Rollo. But I don't like it. Isn't it a bit shabby and unworthy of you, scheming like this just to rob a thief of his stolen money?'

Oh Christ! thought Rollo irritably. The pi little woman! The evangelising angel again!

'Let's get control of that hundred grand first,' he said cheerfully. 'Then we'll argue the ethics and the metaphysics of the situation for as long as you want.'

'If you say so, Rollo. I do hope you know what you're doing.'

'That's a good girl. Meet me outside the Officers' Bar as soon after touch-down as you can make it. I'll have a taxi standing by. We've got until six o'clock this evening to work things out the way we want them.'

He took a biscuit from one of the passenger trays and nibbled it thoughtfully as he looked at Yvonne's icy disapproving profile.

'Just remember, Lady Honesty, you've heard nothing about all this. You observe strict neutrality in our little crusade over the Blackstock inheritance. If you foul up this deal for us, I guarantee you'll come to grief. And I mean grief!'

5

The jetliner made an impeccable approach through the low wooded hills near Basle and lightly touched down on the concrete runway with no more than a puff of burnt rubber smoke from its tyres. Its momentum carried it close to the squat airport buildings and control tower. Then with skilful use of brakes and reverse thrust Rollo brought the plane round and stopped it with its exit door facing the covered way which led to the passengers lounge and customs sheds. The high-pitched whine of the jets faded out in a long diminuendo like a distant wailing siren.

Sally, the flawless, dedicated hostess, was standing radiant at the open door, with her smart tunic buttoned up and her Union Cavalry hat perched elegantly on her blonde hair. She dutifully wished the passengers a pleasant holiday and *bon voyage*, thanking them for flying with Air

Mercury as they filed out down the stairs into the warm sunshine.

Meanwhile Joe Blackstock was taking a cordial farewell of Yvonne Belmondo in the galley.

'Don't forget to look me up if you change your mind about staying on in Basle,' he said with an insinuating wink. 'I'll be staying at the Montana Hotel in the town centre, and I guarantee to give you a marvellous time.'

'*Au revoir*, big boy,' said Yvonne with a bold challenging look. 'Perhaps you get a nice surprise, huh?'

'I'll look forward to it anyway.'

He waited in the aircraft for Rollo to carry out his switching-off and closing-down drill. Sally Crowther gave Joe a warm caressing look as if she'd at last overcome her former indifference and mild hostility towards him. She wished him a happy and successful trip.

'She's come alive! I've got to her at last,' thought Joe triumphantly. 'After several hundred miles of treating me like a bad smell, she's suddenly realised I'm wearing trousers, and Rollo Seaton is not the only man on earth.'

Shortly afterwards he descended from the crew's exit with Rollo and his co-pilot and walked between them into the terminal building without even being noticed by the customs men.

'Bye bye, old son,' said Rollo breezily as he left Joe at the taxi rank. 'Don't do anything I wouldn't do. That leaves you a hell of a healthy margin.'

'Thanks again,' said Joe. 'You've saved my life. I'll be just in time for my appointment. Ciao.'

He signalled to a taxi and drove into the centre of the town, feeling in a holiday mood, yet with that undercurrent of excitement that was part of his life's fulfilment. He always experienced the same uplift whenever his nefarious ventures brought him among the Swiss. He found Swiss bankers so delightfully amoral about the custodianship of possessions. They didn't care if all their depositors were the world's most diabolical crooks, parasites and murderers, as long as they could hold the money and set it to breed.

Swiss bankers asked no embarrassing questions and gave every client the top-line security shield which no snooping policeman or prying tax inspector could ever penetrate. So when some arch villain of international status died after having deposited in Swiss banks several plundered fortunes that nobody knew he had, they naturally became the property of the custodians when nobody else could claim them. Joe occasionally reflected, when in contemplative mood, that that was what would ultimately happen to all his large deposits. He was risking long, demoralising years in a cage merely to help swell further the swollen coffers of the famous financial Gnomes.

The whole atmosphere of the clean bustling town, with its flavour of cosmopolitanism, its garish advertisements for foreign-sounding beers, wines and liqueurs, its hinterland of picture-postcard mountains, couldn't fail to make the repressed Englishman feel he'd slipped his responsible bonds for a spell and left the normal restraints of law behind.

Joe paid off his taxi at the Hotel

Montana, which was centrally situated, not too big to be comfortable, not old enough to be dowdy, not too commercial to give efficient and courteous service. The pretty painted signs affixed to the wall beside the front entrance proclaimed that it was recommended by the various touring organisations of France, Germany, Italy and the U.S.A., as well as by the A.A. and R.A.C.

The Montana was owned and run by the numerous members of one family. One of the younger sons of the third generation had been at the reception desk for as long as Joe could remember. He was a fair-haired, dapper, excessively polite little man in white bow-tie and morning coat whom everyone called Irwin.

A uniformed flunkey stood permanently on guard in the glassed-in vestibule. He had stood there to Joe's knowledge for the past five years. The foyer was close-carpeted in deep wine red and furnished in an opulent old-fashioned way with gilt chairs upholstered in *petit-point*, bulbouslegged tables and rich velvet drapes. The walls were cosily panelled in dark wood and square columns rose to the high ornate ceiling. There were potted palms and various exotic house-plants in every corner.

Irwin greeted Joe Blackstock with deference as a valued customer and gave him the key to Number Seven, the suite he usually occcupied, on the first floor, overlooking the street.

Joe stripped off and had a shower. He was in no hurry to go to the money changers. He could take a few weeks over the transaction if he wanted to, touring Switzerland in leisurely fashion while the Robbery Squad beavered away in increasing frustration back at home. He decided the cash would be safe enough locked in his suitcase inside the wardrobe, with the outer door of his suite locked. Nobody knew he had a large amount of money with him and that was the essential guarantee of its safety. If he played extra safe and asked to deposit his suitcase in the hotel strongroom, it would be an admission that he carried something of real value. Even sober Swiss hoteliers or their family connections and hangers-on were not beyond temptation on the scale that Joe was carrying it.

Feeling ready for an apéritif and a good lunch, and deciding to eat alone in his room, Joe phoned his order down to the kitchen. It came up in twenty minutes, a large Chateaubriand steak with asparagus tops and French fries and a bottle of red wine, followed by an assortment of Swiss cheese and a bowl of fruit from Italy.

Feeling replete and very satisfied with life, Joe flung open the inner and outer french doors and stepped out on to the small balcony overlooking the street. The subdued roar of traffic came up from the sunlit town. The pure September air was warm enough for shirt-sleeves. The façades of shops and hotels looked cleaner than usual against the blue sky and the distant hills. As Joe looked down at the shoppers and tourists strolling in leisurely fashion he reflected that even some of the ant-like Swiss seemed to be taking time off from making money.

Suddenly he noticed a familiar blue uniform on a handsome, long-legged blonde girl with fleshy hips. She was window-shopping on the other side of the street, where every alternate shop seemed to be a prosperous jeweller's, or to have its windows loaded with Swiss watches and cuckoo clocks. He recognised her as Sally Crowther, Rollo Seaton's professional stand-in. Rollo had let her off the leash in Basle, so he must have very urgent business.

The sight of Sally made Joe realise that a good woman's ministrations were all he needed to set the seal on his wellbeing. So he decided to go down and inveigle her up to his room for a pleasant hour or two. It was still only one o'clock and her plane wasn't scheduled to take off again for Gatwick until six-thirty. She was certainly worth a try.

Joe carefully locked the outer door of his suite and ran downstairs and across the street to intercept Sally. She seemed more scared than surprised at seeing him, which was strange because she certainly hadn't been scared of Joe on the plane. Maybe she was feeling a bit guilty because she'd got away from

72

Rollo and was itchy for an adventure.

'I didn't know you were staying in this part of Basle,' she said lamely.

'Where's Rollo?'

'He's gone to see one of his contacts who gives him little packages to take back to England. Don't ask me what's in them. I daren't even think of it.'

The answer rang so true to someone who knew Rollo that Joe accepted it without question.

'Will I do to entertain you while Rollo's getting his priorities right?'

Sally hesitated anxiously, a very nice girl worried by disloyal thoughts towards her one true mate.

'Come on in the hotel and have a drink,' persisted Joe, oozing all his considerable charm.

'No, I'd rather not, thank you,' said Sally with a blush of modesty that made her look twice as sexy. 'I never drink at midday. I was just on my way to have lunch.'

'Oh, I can take care of that,' offered Joe eagerly. 'They do a reasonable lunch at my hotel. Nothing fancy, but the best of

73

basic ingredients. French chef and Swiss hygiene, a formidable combination.'

'Thank you all the same, but I preferred something a bit more interesting. I know a homely little Czech restaurant a few streets away where they do a Wiener Schnitzel that's out of this world.'

'Fine,' retorted Joe. 'I'll come in with you, if you'll have me. I couldn't put Wiener Schnitzel away right now, but I can supply the champagne and the scintillating conversation.'

'That'll be lovely,' said Sally warmly. 'To tell you the truth I'm not really keen on going into these foreign places on my own. There's always some garlic-reeking Romeo who thinks I must be dying for a man.'

'You can't blame them,' said Joe, bang on cue. 'Supposing I think the same?'

She gave him a sidelong friendly look which was definitely not intended to put him off. Joe felt with an uplift of surging triumph that he was home and dry with this one. Rollo had always had a fatuous complacency about his unshakable hold on his women.

'I didn't think you and I would hit it off at all on the trip over,' said Joe as they strolled along companionably. 'You seemed definitely unfriendly.'

'That was because I was scared of you. Rollo had built you up such a formidable reputation, I thought you were one of the Mafia.'

'He was speaking for himself, of course. What do you think now then?'

'Now you seem perfectly normal and human,' replied Sally with an enigmatic smile. 'I feel completely safe with you — in the middle of Basle.'

They reached the Czech restaurant where Sally proposed to have lunch, a picturesque, oak-beamed, low-ceilinged place with a big old clock ticking away obstreperously up one corner. It had the rustic atmosphere of a hostel in the Black Forest.

They sat at a rickety old table in the little dormer window and Joe pressed on with the softening-up process, while Sally pored over the menu with the time-consuming vacillation of a girl stringing a man along.

By chance Joe happened to glance through the latticed window into the street and suddenly he perked up suspiciously as he saw another familiar, blue-uniformed, nylon-legged girl lurking in a shop doorway out of Sally's line of vision. There was no mistaking the round, dumpy figure of Yvonne Belmondo. She was waving and beckoning to him frantically, and pointing with a conspiratorial warning finger at Sally, indicating that she was to be kept in the dark.

Joe felt his hackles rise with the distinct awareness of treachery and intrigue. Something strange and sinister was going on between the two hostesses.

'Excuse me, Sally,' he said politely. 'I've just remembered I'm to make an important telephone call, to fix an appointment with my bank manager. I won't be long.'

'Don't go away,' said Sally eagerly. 'The proprietor will let you use his private telephone.'

But Joe had already gone, bouncing up the two steps and through the rickety curtained door out on to the street. Yvonne crept furtively out of her doorway.

'Go back to your hotel quickly,' she hissed. 'Seaton he is planning to steal your suitcase. He thinks you 'ave a lot of money in it. He says you were one of the bandits who robbed a bank security van in Dulwich yesterday afternoon. Sally she is the bait to take you out of the way for an hour.'

Joe stiffened with rage, not so much at Rollo's diabolical treachery as at his own smug naïveté in underestimating that cunning snake Rollo and swallowing the bait of his proffered tart. As if it could have been coincidence that Sally appeared so conveniently, hawking her mutton right outside Joe's hotel! He wasn't really surprised at Rollo throwing their whole working connection overboard when he judged the stakes were high enough. That was the code by which they'd both lived and done business for countless years.

'Don't say a word about me telling you,' said Yvonne anxiously. 'Seaton he is a 'orrible man with a 'orrible temper. If he finds out I tell you, I will be kaput.'

'Thanks, Yvonne,' said Joe hurriedly. 'I won't forget you for this. Come and see me any time.'

He took off down the street back towards the Montana Hotel, running with the long urgent strides of righteous anger. He was murderous in his resolution to rescue his booty from the jackal.

Yvonne watched him out of sight with a wary eye and then hurried into a telephone kiosk to complete her own arrangements. She always took a highly individualistic and pragmatic line. She had a business partner in Basle called Fifi Lagaillarde, a small-time French crook, con man and jewel thief who regularly did the season in Basle, fleecing the dumb tourists and pinching travellers' cheques from bags in parked cars or women's handbags. He also preyed on rich, elderly, lonely women in dire need of a flatterer and lover, and he spent some happy hours of recreation in convincing nubile schoolgirls that their price was not above rubies. Fifi was prepared to tackle anything large or small in the thieving

78

line with brilliant improvisation.

Yvonne was certainly not going to stand idly by and have Joe Blackstock's mammoth bank haul swiped by Rollo Seaton, who was a greedy swine and would never share honourably with anyone, when she and Fifi could divide the spoils between them as equal business partners.

Never slow in ideas or execution, Yvonne had already been out shopping in Basle and had bought a white fibreglass suitcase identical in size, shape and colour with Joe's. Fifi had taken charge of it and was now lurking near a telephone booth in the vicinity of the Montana Hotel, waiting for Yvonne's signal that Joe was on his way back. Fifi was going to slink into the hotel and follow Joe up to his suite, there to do his slippery legerdemain with the false suitcase and escape in the general confusion, while Joe had his hands full in repelling the foray of the treacherous Rollo Seaton.

6

From his strategic observation post in a taxi parked some way down the street, Rollo saw with gloating satisfaction how Joe came bouncing cockily down the front steps of the Montana, chatted up Sally with his usual high-powered bonhomie and then walked off with her in a cosy tête-à-tête.

Good old Joe! It never fails. Trail a petticoat in front of his eyes and all his faculties are immediately suspended, except one! Rollo sauntered into the Montana and bought himself a large cognac in the bar just off the foyer. The barman was an old ally and fellow twister of Rollo's called Willi. The sight of a couple of Swiss fifty-franc notes was enough to persuade Willi to sneak up to the hotel register on the reception desk and find out the number of Monsieur Blackstock's suite, while Rollo kept Irwin busy at the other end of the desk, discussing the complaints of an imaginary client, a passenger of Air Mercury, who'd actually been able to find fault with the Montana's impeccable service. A supplementary bribe of another hundred Swiss fancs caused Willi to hand over a hotel master key with which Rollo could walk without hindrance into a locked suite.

Rollo finished his drink in leisurely fashion, sauntered round a fat pillar out of sight of Irwin and slunk silently up the heavily carpeted staircase to the first floor. He quickly located Number Seven and let himself in with the master key. He had a swift look round the sitting-room for the big white suitcase, and then went through to the bedroom. He found what he sought in the bottom of the principal wardrobe, grabbed it with the successful hunter's elation and darted for the door.

At that moment the outer door flew open and Joe Blackstock came crashing through, breathing hard and cursing savagely. There was a look in his eye which Rollo couldn't mistake. Joe really meant business and he had a nasty reputation in a punch-up.

Rollo looked round in a panic for something to hit him with, but all he had was the coveted suitcase which he swung ineffectually at Joe's head. Joe brushed it aside and threw a vicious punch, which Rollo stopped with some difficulty. Neither of them wasted breath on recriminations. There was some ferocious in-fighting. Rollo put up a desperate resistance but he was always on the defensive. He had laid too many women for years and his blood-alcohol content was far too high. Joe rapidly battered down his defences and finished him off with a short sharp hook to Rollo's handsome chin.

As he paused for breath and looked down more in sorrow than anger at the vanquished figure of his youthful comrade from the Congo mercenaries, Joe saw out of the corner of his eye that the suitcase full of money, lying disregarded where Rollo had dropped it, was slowly moving away as if under its own power, and another identical white suitcase had materialised beside it. Fifi Lagaillarde who'd been lurking in an alcove in the corridor outside had nipped in to do his stuff, switching cases under cover of the mêlée. He was crouching down behind the bedroom door. Having placed the empty suitcase he was all set to take a powder with the loaded one when Joe chanced to notice the manoeuvre.

At first he thought he was having hallucinations or getting double vision. He couldn't tell which suitcase was which, but he instinctively went for the one that Fifi was edging away. With an oath of rage he flung himself after the dapper little figure in the blue suit, trilby hat and pointed brown and white shoes who was off like a blue streak with the payload, trailing a cloud of cheap perfume. Fifi had a fair turn of speed and might well have made it, but as he shot out on to the landing he collided with Willi the barman.

Willi, having seen Joe Blackstock arrive in such a tearing hurry in the wake of Seaton's mysterious invasion of his

83

room, had concluded that something highly irregular was afoot. Willi held no particular brief either for Seaton or Blackstock, but he smelt the coming battle like an experienced war-horse and thought there might be some pickings for him if he joined in on the winning side.

He arrived outside Number Seven just in time to wreck Fifi's coup. The two men collapsed in a heap and Joe, flinging himself among the tangled bodies, grabbed his suitcase with one hand and Fifi's ankle with the other.

Spitting and snarling like a fighting alley cat, Fifi wrenched himself free, leapt to his feet and launched a vicious kick at Jo's groin which fortunately missed. Then he took off down the stairs. Without slowing down he rushed through the hotel's kitchens and out into the side street where he'd left his beat-up old Citroën 2 CV with its engine ticking over ready for a fast withdrawal.

Joe let him go. He still had his suitcase full of money as well as Fifi's substitute, but he was far from happy. Apart from

Seaton and his whore, some unknown third party was moving in on the money, prepared and organised with monkey tricks like false suitcases, and that was really ominous.

'Do I call the police, M'sieu'?' grunted Willi as he climbed painfully to his feet and dusted himself down.

'No, don't bother,' retorted Joe casually. 'A scandal involving the police won't do the hotel's reputation any good. It's just a private quarrel. Let's forget it.'

He slipped Willi a hundred francs and Willi went back to his bar, outwardly mollified but inwardly determined to keep a sharp eye on Monsieur Blackstock, who had some very strange friends.

Joe went back into the bedroom where Rollo was still out cold. He filled a tumbler with water and dashed it unceremoniously in Rollo's face. The pilot shuddered, groaned and blinked his eyes. Full consciousness returned, but he just lay there like a fallen idol with his usual neat handsomeness ruffled and unhappy. His elegant blue uniform looked a mess, stained with blood and water. His regular features were already puffy and bloodstained from the battering they'd just sustained. He was in no hurry to get to his feet and rejoin battle for the coveted suitcase.

'I don't really blame you for wrecking our beautiful friendship,' said Joe tolerantly. 'After all, a man's trustworthiness depends on his standard of living. What bothers me is how you found out the stakes were high enough on this particular trip.'

Rollo fingered his jaw tenderly and moved it from side to side as if to reassure himself that it hadn't been knocked off.

'You didn't have to hit me so hard, you bastard,' he grumbled. 'I've got lockjaw. I'll get you for this, Blackstock, if it takes me the rest of my life.'

'Don't put yourself out,' replied Joe. 'You and Sally were doing good team-work with the old decoy trick. I must have softening of the brain not to see through that. What I can't figure out is where that other slimy little bugger in the blue suit fits in. He was like an eel bristling with knees and boots.'

'What are you talking about? There

was nobody else here.'

'Oh yes there was. It was a cheeky attempt to switch suitcases. Look here. This empty one is an exact replica. If you'd resisted for another ten seconds he'd have made it. Who was he and how did he know?'

'You're talking cock as far as I'm concerned. That bloody little tramp Yvonne, she tipped you off, didn't she? I'll give her a bloody face-lift. You can depend on it.'

'You're wrong. It wasn't Yvonne. It was Sally's lousy acting. It occurred to me that she was a bit too co-operative and sugary all of a sudden, turning up here to be picked up after giving me the snow treatment on the plane. When I started to wonder why I eventually came up with the answer.'

'You needn't try to cover for that bloody Belmondo,' snarled Rollo viciously. 'I know bloody well it had to be her who got you here so fast.'

'You still haven't told me how you knew I'd got something worth lifting in here.'

'Oh, go to hell!' fumed Rollo, picking up his braided cap and heading for the door. 'Don't show your ugly mug on my aircraft again, or I'll arrange for you to go out through the emergency door as soon as we're depressurised.'

'I'll bear it in mind,' said Joe thoughtfully. 'Give my regards to Sally, and I hope she enjoyed her Wiener Schnitzel. I never had the chance to find out what she's like in bed, but I do know she's a lousy actress. Tell her from me her place is in the home with the three C's, cooking, cleaning and crumpet. She's lost and will come to grief in the world of pure bastards like you and me.'

Rollo's reply was a catlike rictus of hatred as he slunk away like a dishonoured and dissipated ghost.

As soon as he'd gone Joe abstracted five thousand pounds from the suitcase, intending to take it to the money-changers that afternoon. The bulk of the loot in its suitcase he took down to Irwin at the reception desk and asked him to lock it in the hotel's strong-room, a massive old-fashioned vault in the cellar, with a steel door three inches thick, where the liquor supply and other valuables were stored. Joe wasn't taking any more chances on the security of the hotel suite now that Rollo Seaton and other opportunists as yet unknown were moving in like vultures on the jackpot. They were bound to try again. The responsibility of guarding so much loot against unknown resourceful predators was beginning to weigh heavy.

Joe spent the rest of the afternoon going round the money shops in Basle, changing his sterling into francs which he then paid into his numbered account.

The men behind the exchange desks gave him strange veiled looks, no doubt wondering why he'd brought so many pounds to change in Switzerland. Even when exchange controls had been lifted in London it was certainly unusual for a tourist to be in possession of so much English currency when travellers' cheques were so much more convenient in transit.

However, the money men offered no

objection beyond a raised eyebrow or two. Buying pounds a few points below the current exchange rate was good Swiss business and they knew by instinct that this client was in no position to haggle.

7

When Joe returned to his hotel much later in the afternoon, he found Yvonne Belmondo waiting for him in the foyer of the Montana. Her eyes were swollen with tears and she presented a convincing picture of conventional female distress.

She hadn't seen hide nor hair of Fifi since his fiasco with the dummy suitcase. He hadn't shown up at their rendezvous and she was in dreadful suspense, itching to know whether he'd double-crossed her or whether he'd met disaster. If he'd bungled it and been grabbed by the fuzz, he was really on his own. Yvonne would cheerfully let him rot. She made no investment in failure.

She intended to find out what had really happened by pumping Joe Blackstock, but she knew she would have to be extremely subtle in her questioning in order not to reveal that she was one of the predators.

'Hullo, Yvonne,' said Joe, glancing at his watch. 'I thought you were taking off for Gatwick at 18.30. You're going to be a bit pushed now, aren't you?'

'I am not going back,' said Yvonne tearfully. 'I dare not show my face with Air Mercury any more. That Seaton he would kill me for betraying him to you and spoiling his lousy robbery. So I'ave quit my job.'

'Really? Just like that? What are you going to do then? You can't live on fresh air. Even that costs money in Switzerland.'

'I manage somehow,' said Yvonne with restrained nobility. 'Perhaps I get a job with Swissair or Pan American. If not, I'ave to sell myself to some man. *Violà tout*.'

She looked at him with devoted and imploring eyes, willing him to remember the light-hearted offer he'd made to her during the flight when he was merely after crumpet.

'I certainly owe you a lot for tipping me off about Rollo Seaton when Sally had me decoyed,' said Joe. 'You won't have to starve while I'm in Switzerland anyway.'

Yvonne's swimming tears vanished as rapidly as they'd been turned on.

'Oh, thank you, thank you!' she cried ecstatically. 'I always knew you were a good guy in spite of all that Seaton said about you being a gangster. I am so glad you 'ang on to your money.'

'You seem pretty convinced that I'm a walking goldmine,' said Joe bluntly. 'How has word suddenly got around Basle that I'm Croesus?'

'Are you not then? Seaton he knew you'ave a lot of money that you must have stolen from a bank. You'ave given him a big roll of new ten-pound notes to pay for your fare. He said it was'ot money.'

'So that's it,' muttered Joe. 'I must be getting senile not to have foreseen that with Rollo. I'll never make that mistake again. Fifty-pence tips to the tradesmen from now on.'

'*Comment?*'

'It's amazing how money distorts everybody's judgment when big sums are involved,' mused Joe.

'You take me to the cabaret, big boy?' wheedled Yvonne, fondling his hand.

'Later on perhaps. I need a drink after all that aggro with the rats, and then it'll be time for dinner.'

'What really 'appened with you and Seaton?' she said curiously. 'You get back in time?'

'Fortunately yes. Just in time to stop him walking off with my suitcase. We parted bad friends.'

'So. You still 'ave your suitcase?'

'Of course.'

'And what you 'ave inside it?'

'Naturally.'

'Why you say naturally? How are you so certain?'

'What are you getting at, Yvonne?'

'Oh, nothing,' she said lightly. 'You take me to your room now? I think I just like to rest for a time.'

She gave him a smouldering, meaningful look which told him that rest was the last thing she had in mind.

'OK,' said Joe, by no means reluctant. 'Go on upstairs to Number Seven. I'll be right behind you.'

'You still fancy me, big boy?' she murmured, taking his hands and pressing them on her plump breasts. 'I always knew you are the man for me, *chéri*.'

'It's a good thought,' said Joe, his blood-pressure rising fast. 'Let's get on with it.'

Yvonne skipped up the stairs eagerly like a young filly, showing plenty of strong, stocky leg. When they were in the bedroom she threw her clothes off with compulsive haste, and opened her arms to him with genuine hunger. She had a good body, taut, well fleshed, white and unblemished. She was twenty-one, old enough to have considerable experience and young enough still to take a zestful, whole-hearted joy in it. She went at her business like a top-line athlete and taught Joe a couple of new positions before she finally wore him to a standstill. In her own intense pleasure she even forgot momentarily that she was there to rob him.

Joe drifted off into an exhausted sleep with Yvonne's plump young arms clasped tight about him. Yvonne too slept for over an hour to replenish her jaded tissues.

When she awoke feeling refreshed and fulfilled, she remembered the real reason why she was there in that bed with this big gorilla *anglais*. She had to check up on Fifi Lagaillarde.

She gently disengaged herself from Joe's embrace. He groaned, turned over and went on sleeping. Yvonne crept stealthily out of bed and went into the sitting-room, where the empty white suitcase brought in by Fifi was still on a chair. She examined it quickly. It was certainly the one she'd bought, proof that Fifi had delivered it to Blackstock's suite. She went hurriedly through the rooms, opening all the cupboards, looking under all the furniture for Joe's original suitcase, but it wasn't there. Yvonne was frantic with suspense. Had Fifi, the expert thief, got away with the case of loot, or hadn't he?

She started to get dressed hurriedly, determined to find Fifi and have it out with him. She knew enough about Fifi's shifty activities to give him a very rough passage with the gendarmerie if he had double-crossed her.

As she squirmed into her scanty knickers and hauled up her tights, she suddenly became aware that Joe's eyes were fixed on her. He'd been awake for a few seconds, lazily watching her busy activity, and somewhere at the back of his mind the alarm bells were ringing, as positively as if he'd just seen lawmen with a road-block up ahead. Now that he was no longer blinded by sexual desire he could see Yvonne more objectively, and he definitely didn't like what he saw. The way she had gone rooting through his suite as if on some whore's treasure hunt was very off-putting.

Also Yvonne's manner towards him had subtly changed as if she'd lost patience and didn't care whether she offended him or not.

'That suitcase in there,' she said crossly, 'are you sure it is yours?'

'Of course it's mine. I brought it with me from England, and I don't know anybody else who's got title to it.'

'Oh, you are so stupid! 'Ave you checked that what is in it is still in it?'

'Why should I want to do that? It's locked, and nobody but me has the key to it.'

'Open it,' she said impatiently.

'What the hell for?'

'I will soon show you what for. Give me the key.'

Joe climbed out of bed in leisurely fashion, hauled on his trousers and tossed her the key.

'You see?' cried Yvonne triumphantly. 'It does not fit. This is not your suitcase.'

'Now I wonder how you worked that out,' said Joe imperturbably.

The mystery of the slippery little sneak thief who'd so nearly succeeded in switching the suitcase was a mystery no longer.

'Do you not see, you imbecile?' cried Yvonne, shrill and ugly with rage. 'You 'ave been tricked. Somebody 'as changed your full suitcase for this empty one. And you never even noticed, you great fool!'

'You'd better get after the creep,' said Joe coolly. 'He might have spent it all by now. I want that key back, by the way, even though your thieving friend has got my suitcase.'

She threw it at him with a blasphemy and turned to go.

'Oh, just one other thing,' said Joe, flinging a five-franc coin at her feet. 'That's for the ride, you miserable French shit!'

Yvonne unleashed a torrent of multi-lingual obscenity that made him raise his eyebrows in mild surprise. Then she stormed out of his suite and out of the hotel to look for Fifi. At least she'd found out what she came to find: Fifi had failed to switch cases. Joe Blackstock must still have the money in some safe deposit, or he wouldn't have been so smug and superior. It was a pity she'd had to betray her collusion with Fifi, but it was the only way to find out. Blackstock was so secretive and Fifi was such a bloody liar. She would have to join forces with him to work out another plan of campaign. Blackstock was bound to be on the move across Switzerland with his haul before long. He dare not change too much sterling in one town or he might attract the attention not only of the police but of other Swiss entrepreneurs ambitious to dispossess him. He would probably go on to Zurich next. That was the logical place for a money man.

Joe got dressed and had a peaceful dinner in the hotel restaurant. Then he set off into the less salubrious quarters of Basle where he had a few valuable contacts among the sub-community. Here there were narrow streets of old wooden houses with wide, overlapping eaves like dolls' houses, and bright patches of colour from geraniums in window-boxes.

He made his way to a beer cellar where the patron, Klaus Kretchmer, was a former German member of the French Foreign Legion and operated a black market in all the forbidden merchandise and accessories constantly needed by the criminal community.

For two thousand francs Joe purchased a nine-millimetre Walther automatic pistol, a box of ammunition and a bullet-proof vest. This was a close-knit texture of tough nylon twine and strands of highly tempered steel, reinforced with supple steel bands. Now that Yvonne had obviously spread the news of Joe's jackpot among her crooked contacts in Basle, Joe was going to need all the hardware he could get.

His plan was to go down the central valley to Zurich and make a leisurely tour of the big cities, Bern, Lucerne, Geneva, changing a few thousand in each place until it was all converted. Normally he didn't like using firearms. Their work was too irrevocable, too incriminating, and attracted too much in the way of energetic countermeasures from the law. But with the amount of cash he was known to be carrying, he accepted that the enemy would stop at nothing.

The bullet-proof vest should be some guard against the surprise factor and give him a second chance. He knew it wouldn't stop high-velocity bullets at close range, but he was banking on the fact that conventional thieves and murderers generally carried small-to medium-calibre side-arms, against which his body armour would provide adequate protection. They might shoot him in the head of course. That was always a danger to be accepted when hoodlums used live ammunition. But he was conditioned to embrace the calculated risk that belonged to the game.

From Fifi's antics with the dummy suitcase, Joe concluded that he wouldn't make the second team in any racket. But there was no knowing what kind of reinforcements he might be able to dredge up.

It might have been safer and wiser to leave the cash where it was, in the hotel strong-room, for a week or two in the hope that the gathering vultures would give up and disperse. But even that course had its obvious dangers. The longer he delayed the longer his enemies would have to gather their forces and co-ordinate an attack. They would never give up as long as they knew that amount of currency was sitting under their noses. A mere hotel strong-room wouldn't deter them for long. Strong-rooms were made to be cracked open by the enterprising. Moreover, even Irwin or some other member of the Montana's proprietorial family who had access to the strong-room might start getting ideas for improving their status. The Pope himself might seek a little dispensation for two hundred grand, tax-free. There was no question but that the boldest course, as always, was the best. Joe took a certain pride in his own consistency.

8

The following morning after an excellent night's sleep Joe had a leisurely breakfast of fruit, coffee and hot croissants and then telephoned a car-hire firm for a self-drive car. Although it would be quicker by rail to Zurich, he'd decided that a man alone in a train is a sitting duck for bushwhackers. The marked-out victim can be coshed or stabbed and brusquely parted from his property, with the attacker scurrying away to get lost among the other passengers before anybody has noticed anything unusual.

On the other hand a man driving his own car, constantly alert for danger, is a formidable opponent and difficult to rob. The mere possession of a pistol made him feel like a man with an extra pair of balls.

He was wearing his bullet-proof vest under his shirt. It came down well below his navel and its chunky, restrictive enclosure of his torso gave him a tremendous feeling of confidence, even though it was going to make the sweat boil out of him by midday.

Before he set out he took the precaution of stuffing as much money as possible into all his pockets, about ten thousand pounds. The rest of the cash he split evenly between the two identical suitcases, so that in the event of the opposition wresting one suitcase from him and leaving him alive, he would still have half the haul left.

On the floor of his rented Peugeot 504 under his legs he placed his own suitcase, and close to his right hand on the seat, hidden by the morning's newspaper, was the Walther automatic with a full magazine and a round in the breech. The second suitcase, presented to him by Yvonne through Fifi, was locked in the boot of the car.

It was a fine, clear morning with a chill refreshing breath coming off the mountains. The early sun shone on the rosetinted peaks with their pines and eternal rocks below the snow-line.

The golden rays glowed richly on the burnished fruit of apple trees in Swiss cottage gardens as he headed out down the valley on the pleasant run to Zurich. It was a day of green and gold. He felt strangely elated with the sure expectation of danger. Let the marauding rats come on. He was ready for anything.

He'd done about twenty miles at a leisurely speed and several cars had overtaken him, any combination of which could have contained the opposing team. The ambush was sprung on an isolated stretch of road a kilometre past a village.

As he came up a fairly steep incline which conveniently checked his speed, and entered a gloomy clump of trees, a large black Opel Manta with two men in it shot out of a side road and tangled with him, forcing him on to the leaf-strewn verge. He had to brake and stop abruptly in order to avoid smashing himself up against a tree. Although he'd been expecting the attack, he was still shaken by its sudden violence.

The Opel stopped a couple of yards

away and two men leapt out, cosmopolitan hoodlums of Fifi's fraternity from the slums of Basle, known respectively as Stavros and Giacopo.

Stavros, a punch-drunk Greek muscle man, rushed to Joe's door and attacked him viciously with an iron bar, while Giacopo, sleek, swarthy and fastidiously overdressed, ran round to the door on the other side and dived in to snatch the suitcase.

Joe parried Stavros's first blow with the barrel of his pistol and then slashed the Greek across the face with it. Stavros reeled back and, seeing that he was likely to get his head blown off, ran away and took cover behind a tree, setting up the quarry for Giacopo's pistol. As Joe charged after Stavros he heard the crack of a pistol shot and felt a sharp, violent blow between his shoulder-blades. He knew then with fierce satisfaction that his armoured vest had been a sound investment.

He caught up with Stavros, parried another murderous swing with the iron bar and jabbed the Greek hard in the solar plexus with his pistol barrel. Joe's main sensory impressions of Stavros were a sickening smell of fried onions and olive oil, a hairy pelt like a gorilla's and dirty finger-nails on blunt, massive hands. As Stavros doubled up, winded by the jab in his guts, Joe landed him a crack in the head with his pistol and the big Greek subsided with a groan.

When Stavros was out of the line of fire, two more pistol shots went off and two more bullets whacked against Joe's steel waistcoat, causing him to stagger under the impact. Giacopo was a good shot with his 7.65 millimetre and he couldn't understand why his target didn't go down. At that moment Joe could have shot him easily, but he knew there would be police on the scene before long and he didn't want the extra complication of being thrown into a Swiss gaol for shooting a small-time crook.

The next event was that Fifi Lagaillarde, who'd been jogging along half a mile behind Joe in his wheezing 2 CV, came to join the affray. Appraising the situation swiftly he sneaked round behind a tree and came at Joe from the rear. He drove a vicious knife thrust hard between Joe's shoulder-blades and then howled with pain and rage as the point met an impenetrable steel barrier, jarring his wrist and arm to the shoulder with numbing force. Fifi hurriedly withdrew to a safe distance to nurse his pain.

Giacopo had now caught on to the idea of the bullet-proof vest and was coldly and painstakingly drawing a bead on Joe's head. Things were getting serious now. Joe flung himself flat on the leafy ground, rolled over a couple of times and loosed off two quick shots at Giacopo. They both missed and the target shimmered hurriedly behind a tree.

The affair looked like freezing into a dangerous stalemate. But then Stavros, who was as tough as old hickory, recovered from his stunned condition and teamed up with Fifi to make a two-pronged attack through the trees. As they both rushed him, Joe shot Fifi through the shoulder. Giacopo dare not shoot now for fear of hitting his own men. Stavros reached Joe from the other direction before he could swing his pistol into an aiming position. A heavy boot thudded viciously into his ribs and once again his steel vest saved him from serious injury. Stavros then kicked the pistol out of Joe's hand and the two men closed together like tearing, snarling wild cats.

Fifi was bleeding like a stuck pig from his dangerous shoulder wound and screaming raucously with fear. Giacopo forgot everything else and rushed over to him to try to stem the bleeding.

A passing motorist had stopped beside the two damaged vehicles to offer assistance, but as soon as he heard the shots and saw the brutal mêlée raging under the trees, he took off again with frenzied haste to find the police.

At the height of the confusion Yvonne Belmondo, who'd been following Fifi in a hired Volkswagen Beetle, pulled up alongside Joe's Peugeot. She took in the situation at a glance like a true opportunist: Joe and Stavros rolling over and over, battering each other like maniacs; Fifi bleeding copiously from a gunshot wound, and Giacopo desperately trying at the same time to fix a tourniquet and keep the blood off his own snazzy suit. They were all far too busy to notice Yvonne's arrival.

It took a matter of seconds for her to verify that Giacopo had pinched what she thought was the decoy suitcase and to conclude that the geniune jackpot was inside the locked boot. She snatched the ignition key from the switch under the steering-wheel and rushed round to unlock the boot. In a few seconds she'd snatched up Joe's second suitcase, thrown the Peugeot's ignition key away among the trees and rushed back to her own car with the spoils. Then she roared off at full speed down the road to Zurich.

Joe heard the frenzied clatter of her engine as he buried his knee in Stavros's pendulous guts. But Stavros, a glutton for punishment, wouldn't let go. Then by sheer good fortune Joe managed to retrieve his own pistol from where it had fallen among the leaves. In desperation he shot Stavros point-blank through the chest, the only way to get clear of him. Looking round he was just in time to

111

see the beetle-shaped rear of Yvonne's car disappear down the road. He also saw that the boot of his Peugeot was wide open with the suitcase gone and the ignition key also missing.

He cursed furiously as he realised that Yvonne had outsmarted them all. If only he'd used his initial advantage and shot all three of the international consortium straight-away instead of pussyfooting around trying to avoid killing anybody, this disaster would never have happened.

He rescued the second suitcase, flung it into the Opel Manta and climbed in after it. Then he was off in hot pursuit of Yvonne. But she had a good start. She drove with reckless and furious skill on that winding road, knowing that Joe would mess her up for good if he caught her. Joe never had another glimpse of the fawn-coloured Volkswagen. In the small township of Frick she turned off down a side street and lost herself in a maze of minor roads among the villages, while Joe went pounding straight through on the road to Zurich. He tried to think ahead of Yvonne and outguess her.

'She won't dare show her face in Basle again after double-crossing those three hoodlums. Knowing I'm on her tail she'll want to be out of Switzerland as fast as possible.'

He thought she was sufficiently French to look to France as her spiritual home, and with a load of money in her possession she would think automatically of Paris. That would seem to indicate the Simplon Orient Express from Switzerland to Paris as soon as she could make it. Joe was resolved to catch up with her if it took him the rest of his life. If he allowed her to get away unscathed with half his haul, he would never be able to live with himself. His professional pride would never recover from the ignominy. Nor would he be able to face Vic Mannion and tamely admit that half the proceeds of the Dulwich operation had been filched from him with ludicrous, child-like ease by a French tart he'd been to bed with, a pathetic little nothing of a foul-mouthed slut.

9

In hot pursuit of Yvonne Belmondo Joe drove straight to the railway station at Zurich and waited for the Simplon Orient Express to Paris. He had a strong gut feeling that Yvonne would try to get aboard it. But though he laboriously scanned all the faces waiting on the long platform and in the buffets and bars, though he went up and down the waiting train peering hard into every carriage, there was no sign of his quarry.

In fact Yvonne had driven by a circuitous route to the German border and crossed the frontier near Schaffhausen. Her passport was in order. She said she was a French tourist and flashed her dazzling white teeth in a lovely smile at the frontier guards. They let her through with a perfuctory stamping of her passport and an incurious glance into her car. They expressed no wish to open up the single white suitcase on the back seat.

She drove down the *Autobahn* to Frankfurt and then crossed the French frontier with equal ease. The following day she arrived uneventfully in Paris and went to stay for a few days with her mother, who lived in a poor way in a oneroom flat in the outer suburbs. Giselle Belmondo was still legally an old maid, even though she'd been common-law wife to several men.

Joe meanwhile was proceeding with the essential task of changing the remaining money into francs and paying it into his Swiss account. He kept nimbly on the move all over Switzerland and used a number of aliases, for he knew the Swiss police would have traced his hiring of the Peugeot and would be anxious to question him about that fracas in the woods in which two men had been shot. When the money was all successfully banked he returned to Basle in disguise and set about uncovering Yvonne's tracks.

A few telephone calls told him which car-hire firm had rented a fawn-coloured VW Beetle on September 5th to a short dark French girl known as Yvonne

Belmondo. She'd hired it for a week and paid cash in advance, so they weren't bothered for the present where she'd taken it. By bribing the manager Joe succeeded in finding out the address to which the car had been delivered.

It was a small, respectable, clean house in the unfashionable part of Basle, owned by a widow woman in reduced circumstances. She let her two spare rooms to paying guests and Yvonne always stayed there when she had an overnight stay in Basle.

Joe told the woman he was a flight controller from Air Mercury, Mademoiselle Belmondo's English charter company, and had called to collect some flight schedules which Yvonne had forgotten to take with her. He was playing a long shot in assuming that Yvonne in her hurried departure would have left some belongings there, and it turned out he was right. Yvonne's eagerness to be in at the ambush sprung by Fifi and his team meant that the single room, still on hire to Yvonne, was littered with her possessions.

Whether the old woman believed his plausible tale or was merely intimidated, Joe didn't know or care. She led him upstairs to a small white-painted bedroom, cosily furnished and adorned with old dark engravings of Swiss mountain scenery. She invited him to look for the papers he wanted and quietly left him to it. Whatever Mademoiselle Belmondo had to do with this too-polite Englishman with the cold eyes, she didn't want to get mixed up in it.

Yvonne was evidently an untidy little slut who left her clothes, shoes, underwear and toilet requisites all jumbled together in the most unpredictable places. Joe sorted them out methodically, looking above all for letters from friends or relatives which might contain addresses where she could have gone to ground.

Yvonne did not leave her correspondence lying around, so he drew blank there. What he did find in a drawer underneath some sexy underwear were some newspaper articles in French, cut out of *Le Figaro*. A cursory glance told him they were all political articles with a strong rightwing nationalistic bias. They predicted woe and damnation from the recent wild leap into socialism taken by the fickle and mercurial French electorate. Their other common factor was that they were all written under the byline of a certain Alain Doumont. Evidently he was a journalist in whom Yvonne took a considerable personal interest. Would she have cut out and saved so reverently a series of arid chauvinistic newspaper articles because she was a politically motivated French intellectual? Joe did not think so. With an earthy, pragmatic, hot-tailed bitch like Yvonne it must be the man and not the journalist who provoked and sustained her interest. Alain Doumont, God help him! was her hero and probably her lover, assumed Joe. The dates at the top of the newspaper cuttings were fairly recent, so Alain must be still in favour. Joe realised it was the strongest lead he would ever find, and he judged it good enough. Locate Alain Doumont, political correspondent of *Le Figaro*, and Yvonne with Joe's hundred thousand

118

pounds sterling would eventually home in on him.

So Joe bought a good supply of French francs and took a plane for Paris. Arriving there on a hot September afternoon, he took a taxi to the Rue Corbera and hired a room for an indefinite stay at the Hotel Lux. This was a seven-storey modern building of cosmopolitan flavour, catering almost exclusively for foreign tourists. Though not exactly luxurious or in a very fashionable district, it was within walking distance of the Gare de Lyon and only a few minutes' ride by taxi from the centre of playtime Paris. At the Hotel Lux an Englishman would not stand out like a sore thumb, for parties of them were always coming and going.

Joe was not in a feverish hurry to find Yvonne. He was philosphically resigned to the fact that she would probably have spent a considerable sum of the money by the time he caught up with her, and he would take it out on her hide *pro rata*. The only really important thing now was that she didn't get away with it and thus become a running sore to his machismo.

Professional pride was such an obsession with him that he couldn't bring himself to ring up Vic Mannion and report his progress with banking the money until he'd caught up with Yvonne and thus had no shameful excuses to make to his partner. Meanwhile, in the course of the pursuit he was going to enjoy Paris as a holiday-maker in sunny September, when it was still warm enough to sit out on the pavement under the awnings, and the bright lights were at their peak for the season of frivolity.

10

Back in Hampstead Vic Mannion had just taken possession of Joe Blackstock's car, which had been located in the Gatwick visitors' car park and driven away by Rex Roberts, Vic's factotum and general handyman. Rex was a tough, square, stockily built man in his late twenties, an ex-paratrooper who'd done his few stints in Northern Ireland and was stoically resigned thereafter to meeting any kind of aggravation in the line of duty. His great asset in Vic's eyes was that he had no criminal record, so Vic could relax without the nagging fear of having mean-eyed lawmen snooping around the place to check up on some real or imagined petty crime committed by Rex. In fact Vic wouldn't have given employment to anybody with as much as a traffic conviction to his name. He was so acutely aware of his social standing as one of the Hampstead élite that any domestic worker even slightly reminiscent of Vic's hard-working past was to be avoided like the plague.

'Here she is then, Guv'nor,' said Rex in his cheerful cockney voice. 'JB 2 you said was her number. Goes like a dream, as long as you don't think about the tab when you pull up at the pumps.'

Vic looked dubiously at the bright-red Jaguar XJS. It was a very sexy motor, a bit too flashy for his own taste and with far too much power to be practicable for everyday motoring in and around London. But it suited Joe all right and went well with his image of the younger, speed-mad man-about-town with money to burn. No doubt it helped him to pull the birds and impress the socialites, which must mean a great deal in Joe's scale of values.

As he walked round the car and thought back uneasily to the reason why it was there, Vic felt an instinctive dread of it. It brought his mind back with a jolt to the fearful duty that was laid upon him, his pledge to Joe Blackstock to infiltrate an expert assassin into Walthamstow

Police Station and immediately forestall the impending betrayal by the captured criminal who had no loyalty except to his own survival.

The more he thought about the formidable enterprise, the more defeated and depressed Vic became. To kill a man in custody right down in the heart of a London Police Station! All Vic's ageing wisdom prompted the conviction that it couldn't be done, even though he was prepared to splash money about right and left in the attempt. Just suppose that the daring mission failed and the assassin was captured in Walthamstow Police Station. What about the risk of his trading information with the fuzz for a lighter sentence?

With the gathering menace of Tom Garbutt putting Joe Blackstock in the frame, how would Vic Mannion stand if the fuzz should somehow find out that he was looking after Joe's car while he was off on some dubious business abroad? They would certainly get the idea that he and Blackstock had a deal of business activity in common. They would start digging and poking around to uncover some tangible criminal association, and who could tell what they might come up with?

However, the odds against their ever finding Joe's car in Vic's possession must be too great to constitute a serious menace. Keeping the Jaguar was a small enough risk for Vic to take compared with the hazardous enterprise Joe had undertaken to export the full load of stolen money to Switzerland. But it seemed a bit Irish for Joe to worry about the safety of a mere fifteen-thousand-quid car when he'd just successfully stolen two hundred grand. There was no accounting for a man of Joe's education forming an attachment to a piece of replaceable machinery.

Vic got in the Jaguar and looked carefully in the glove compartment to make sure Joe had left nothing incriminating there. Then he looked in the back seat, walked round to the rear and opened the boot. There was absolutely nothing on view to excite a policeman or even a casual thief.

'It'll be OK, I suppose,' said Vic. 'Drive it into the back of the garage and throw a dust-sheet over it. Then bring me the key. We shouldn't have to store it for long anyway.'

'Right-o, guv.'

Rex got in the car, started up and drove round to the large garage at the side of the house where there was room for half a dozen cars. At present it contained the eminently practical Ford Cortina which Vic used, and the Toyota Starlet which Vic had bought for Erika.

Shortly afterwards Vic set out alone to keep the appointment he'd set up with a recommended hit-man, the best in the business, to eliminate Tom Garbutt before he told all he knew. The meeting had been arranged by an old business associate of Vic's, who had himself used the assassin successfully. It was to take place in the bar of a pub called The Fox and Goose in a shabby district near Holborn Viaduct.

The assassin's name was Sam Junior, an expatriate American who'd plied his grisly trade in the States for years, until the Feds got on his track and he was forced in dire emergency to take a prolonged vacation in Europe. Even though he didn't advertise, a man with a vital skill to offer soon has humanity beating a path to his door. Men of wealth and consequence in London who needed a rival or a partner or a spouse removed without themselves coming under police interrogation, soon got to know about Sam Junior. He was outrageously expensive, but he was worth it for he was the very best and he left no tracks behind. His methods of execution were diverse and ingenious, so that no particular modus operandi could be said to belong exclusively to Sam Junior, like the artist's signature on a piece of work which characterises lesser criminals.

Vic had been told to be in the public bar at one o'clock with a folded copy of *The Times* under his left arm, and he would be contacted. The pub was busy, especially at the food counter, with a motley collection of office workers, travellers, the unemployed and unemployable, and numerous men like

Vic himself who didn't fit overtly into any category.

Vic bought himself a double Scotch and sat on a bar stool, as isolated as he could contrive to be, with the flying darts and bar billiards constituting a physical hazard all round him, and with the folded *Times* still under his left arm. When he'd been there about ten minutes a man in his thirties, casually dressed in tan trousers, yellow sweat-shirt and open-toed sandals set his Martini-glass on Vic's table and pulled up a stool. His face was sallow and hollow-cheeked with the unhealthy pallor of a man who spent too long in a closed-in, stuffy atmosphere under artificial lighting. His eyes were cold, calculating slits and his mouse-coloured hair was crew-cut so that he looked like an American service man in civvies.

'Is that *The Times* you got there, Mac?' he enquired with a distinctive American accent.

'Sure,' said Vic. 'It's my badge of identification.'

'Is that right? You must be Mr

Mannion then, the guy with the problem.'

'A removal problem,' rejoined Vic promptly. 'And you must be the removal man.'

'You got the down-payment?'

Vic took a bulky envelope from his breast pocket which contained a thousand pounds in twenty-pound notes. The Yank gave them a cursory glance and put the envelope down on the table under his hand.

'So tell me about the mark,' he said forthrightly. 'Name, address, place of work, social habits, like where he goes in his leisure time; a good physical description, or better still a recent photograph.'

'His name's Tom Garbutt. I don't have a photograph of him, but he's six foot three and well built. He's a heavy villain and looks the part, a really ugly bugger. His home address and social habits don't matter because he's in stir, Walthamstow Police Station. We know he's being held there in the cells on a murder rap.'

The assassin stared at him, his cold eyes contracting to even narrower slits.

128

'You mean you need somebody to go in the slammer and waste him there so he can't give evidence?'

'That's it,' said Vic tensely. 'Can you do it? I'll pay absolute top rates.'

'Well, I don't know,' mused the hit-man. 'Its done in the States often enough, even when some Cosa Nostra fink is in Federal custody. But it's a different ball game over here, all these goddamned crazy old-fashioned methods you got. Walthamstow Police Station, you say?'

'Yes, it's not exactly Sing Sing or Alcatraz.'

'Yeah, I guess there has to be a way in and a way out, and no high-grade technological security. But it's in the high-risk category, you understand. It'll cost an extra five grand.'

'That's all right,' said Vic hastily. 'The bastard's got to be put down before he blabs everybody into stir.'

'Half in advance and half when this Garbutt's been blown away,' said Junior briskly.

Vic handed over another bulkier envelope which he'd brought in anticipation.

'How soon can you do it? Speed is vital.'

'No tight time schedule, especially on this assignment,' said the hit-man bluntly. 'Leave it up to me, right? I got to figure a way round all this. If I goof off I'll finish up in the slammer, and maybe get deported back to the States. That's bad medicine for me right now.'

'How will I know when Garbutt's been taken care of?' persisted Vic. 'The fuzz are not likely to put out a communiqué that a prisoner's just been wasted down in the cells.'

'Leave me your telephone number,' replied the hitman. 'I'll give you a ring when it's AOK, and just say, 'Santa Claus is come to town'.'

'And what if it's not AOK?'

'No news is bad news. You better leave town fast. It'll mean I've joined this Garbutt as a guest of the fuzz in the slammer, so you don't have to pay me the other half.'

11

It was Saturday night in Walthamstow and the busy pubs were closing after intensive business. There were sing-songs, arguments and punch-ups out in the streets, with some merely shedding their load of expensive beer, and others shedding blood and teeth in isolated, squalid little brawls. The divisional police, fully stretched as usual, were in their typical quandary, lurking round corners close to the trouble spots, unsure whether to go in hard to clear the streets and be accused of provocation, or whether to keep out of the way and hope the drunken revelry would eventually subside without any severe damage to property.

The decision was made for them in a shopping arcade a few streets away from the Police Station, when a mob of young blacks suddenly smashed the windows of a TV and video parlour and started running off in different directions with the costly machines. In another street close by, a multi-racial commando from Rent-A-Mob overturned a car and set it on fire, while their hangers-on smashed their way into an off-licence and started handing out the bottles of hard stuff into eager hands.

All available police on duty rushed to the scene in an attempt to control the anarchy. They were met by a barrage of missiles, stones, bottles, dustbin lids, and several of the unprotected constables went down with head and facial injuries. There was a desperate call for reinforcements and the Special Patrol Group to contain the mad eruption of violence that was spreading like a forest fire.

Soon the Police Station was denuded of all but a skeleton staff, a sergeant on the desk in the front office and a young constable manning the switchboard in the Communications Room, as everybody else rushed out to the support of their embattled colleagues.

It was then that a filthy old vagrant with lank grey hair and dirt-engrained skin under his bedraggled beard came reeling into the Police Station. His clothes were so old, ragged and plastered with filth that they might have been stripped off a rotting corpse. The assorted stinks that came from him were as revolting as the miasmas rising from a festering garbage tip on a hot day. On broken shoes he shuffled with the reeling gait of a drunk, and tipsily waved an uncorked bottle a quarter full of methylated spirit.

'Hey there, Sarge, how do I get myself arrested?' he mumbled through hiccups. 'The streets ain't safe for a decent man out there. Bang me up in a cell for the night, willya? It ain't much to ask.'

'Get the hell out of here, you bloody old scarecrow!' yelled the desk sergeant, averting his face in revulsion as the medley of stinks got to him. 'Go on! Clear off!'

'That ain't very friendly, Sarge,' hiccupped the old tramp. 'Them black bastards out there looting and burning everything, you'll find them a cosy cell to sleep in and a good breakfast in the morning. But me, who ain't never done anybody no harm — '

'Out, I said! Hop it, you filthy old bastard!'

'So what do I have to do to get put in a cell then, Sarge? Piss on your nice clean floor, or throw my bottle through your nice big window?'

'Please get lost,' implored the exasperated sergeant. 'Can't you see we've got all the trouble we can handle?'

'A peaceful night's sleep, off of the street in a safe cell where no bastard can get at me. That's all I'm asking. And I know I've only got to break the frigging law to get there. One, two, three — '

His arm went back preparatory to throwing his bottle at the window.

'Oh, for Christ's sake!' exclaimed the sergeant desperately.

He put his head through a doorway and called to his colleague on the switchboard.

'Copplestone, leave that bloody phone to ring for a bit, and come and take charge of this bloody old flea-bag for me. Get the keys from the Guv'nor's office and take him down to the cells. The other customers will just have to hold their noses all night. Serve 'em bloody well right!'

Holding the cell keys on their large steel ring, P.C. Copplestone came out and grabbed the festering tramp by the arm, trying to avert his face from the appalling stink.

'Come on then, grandad. It's burying you need, not banging up in a cell.'

'God bless you, sonny,' mumbled the vagrant, clinging affectionately to his arm and allowing himself to be steered along the passage into the secret bowels of the Police Station. Here a locked cage door of stout iron bars opened on to a flight of steep stone steps leading down to the cells.

As they reached the bottom of the steps, the tramp overdid his stumbling act and lurched heavily against the young constable. The sagging side pocket of his baggy coat swung round and something very hard and heavy pressed with sharp edges against the constable's thigh.

P.C. Copplestone was not too young to have developed his copper's nose, nor yet so old, experienced and blasé as to

135

let something go in order to save himself possible trouble. He quickly shoved his hand into the big poacher's pocket of the tramp's coat and encountered the hard cold steel of a short-barrelled Colt Cobra .38, fitted with a silencer.

Immediately the staggering, helpless old vagrant became a frenzied wild cat. He struck the young constable to the ground, jumped on him and knocked him cold with a savage karate blow delivered to the carotid artery in his neck. Then he snatched up the heavy turnkey's ring containing mortise keys to the cell doors and rushed into the brick-lined vaults.

There were eight cells, four on each side. Three of them stood empty with their doors wide open, showing a crude steel bedstead anchored to the concrete, and a stained lavatory without a seat lurking in the far corner. Five of the cells were occupied with their locked flat steel doors facing uncompromisingly outward.

'Garbutt!' hissed the vagrant. 'Which of you is Tom Garbutt? Hurry up, you mother! I'm here to spring you. We can't hang about.'

But Garbutt, lying awake on his urine-stained mattress, had heard the sudden flurry of violence, the savage blows and the choked-off cry of the constable. He knew instinctively that something highly illegal was going on right at the heart of this citadel of the law. When he heard his own name called out he froze with terror, knowing what he knew and the dangerous bargaining power it gave him. Nobody was going to take the risk of breaking into a Police Station to liberate Tom Garbutt for love of him. Some highly paid specialist must have been briefed. Tom Garbutt knew why and by whom. He cowered down on his flock mattress, petrified with fear, hardly daring to breathe as he heard a key being turned roughly in the cell door next to his, which was then flung open.

The inmate was a child-molester, a scrawny, sandyhaired little civil service clerk called Christopher Shilton, charged with indecent assault on eight-and nine-year-old boys and remanded in custody pending reports on him by his shrink.

'Are you Garbutt?' demanded the

rough, uncouth voice.

'No, dear. I'm Christopher,' lisped the queer in soft seductive tones. 'But I'd like to get out of here all the same, if you're offering. Thanks ever so much.'

With an oath the intruder slammed the door on him, relocked it and moved to the next cell. Just then however P.C. Scovell, freshly battered and panting from the front line, came through the cage door, shoving a sullen and battered young West Indian in front of him. Scovell was the biggest, fattest copper on the station, known to his colleagues as The Slob. He was a standing joke among them for the amount of grub he could put away and the fact that he was always hungry. Now, minus his helmet, with a cut on his brow and his uniform fouled with the garbage that had been flung at him, he'd recognised among his tormentors the face of a habitual criminal called Luke Daley, mugger, pickpocket and vandal. As it was impossible to arrest Daley under normal circumstances without causing a Brixton-type race war, Scovell had seized the heaven-sent opportunity to go in and winkle him out when he spotted him slinking away up a side street with a looted video recorder. Daley was bang to rights for once in his life.

When P.C. Scovell pushed open the cage door to the cells and took in the scene below, P.C. Copplestone lying unconscious on the stone floor and a foul-looking scarecrow trying frenziedly to select the right key for one of the cell doors, the fat copper leapt into action. He pushed Luke Daley headlong down the steps in front of him as a sort of battering-ram aimed at the vagrant and charged along in his wake.

By the time the intruder had realised his danger and groped desperately for his revolver, the two-man assault team cannoned into him and knocked him flying. P.C. Scovell jumped on him with his eighteen-stone mass and his ham-like fist rose and fell till the violent struggles ceased with a strangled groan and the vagrant lay insensible. Thoughtfully P.C. Scovell picked up the revolver and dropped it in his pocket. He dragged his highsmelling victim into one of the empty cells and locked the door on him. Then he pushed the terrified Luke Daley into an adjoining cell and locked him in also. Only then did he remember the main reason why he'd made an opportunity to come back to the station from the front line. He had a clutch of ham sandwiches and a trio of cream doughnuts in his locker, for he always got hungry on the eight-to-twelve shift, and getting the filthy end of a street riot made him even hungrier.

12

Detective Chief Superintendent Roy Pritchard of Scotland Yard's Robbery Squad was a tall sardonic man with a cool off-hand manner and he always dressed immaculately to face his clientele. He never lost his temper or became flustered even with the most fatuous blunders of his underlings or the variable misfortunes which beset his investigations from time to time. He always kept his steady, inflexible purpose to get at the whole truth, which is what he'd been trying to do with Tom Garbutt ever since that villain had had the poor taste to get fingered on a murder charge.

But Tom Garbutt, briefed by the cunning Reuben Levine, had been in no hurry to yield up his precious information as Supergrass. He was holding out for the murder charge to be dropped altogether and for him to receive his liberty, a new identity overseas and an inflation-proof pension to keep him in comfort for the rest of his life. All the chief superintendent was empowered to offer him was that the murder charge might be reduced to one of involuntary manslaughter and that Garbutt would not be indicted for the robberies he admitted to, provided that he named all the men he'd worked with and the organisers who'd set up the crimes. The new identity could be arranged for his future safety, but any notion of a sinecurist pension from the Paymaster General was definitely a non-starter. There was no money in it for the Supergrass.

Negotiations were continuing, but they'd reached an acrimonious impasse with neither detective nor villain able to secure the terms he wanted. Then came the bungled attempt of the Saturday-night assassin to get at Tom Garbutt with a revolver and the whole atmosphere of the discussions was radically transformed.

'Well now, Tom,' said the chief superintendent genially, when the villain was brought up once more into the Interview Room, 'I understand you had a bit of excitement down in the cells the other night.'

'You know bloody well what it was all about,' replied Garbutt bitterly. 'I'm a sitting duck down there. I got a right to be protected. I want to be moved to another nick where nobody knows I'm at.'

'We're going to move you as soon as you supply some evidence that you're worth moving. But up to now you've not told us a damned thing that we can move on. Assuming that the Saturday-night business was an assassination attempt aimed at you as a Supergrass, have you any idea who set it up?'

'Course I know. The bastard! He thinks he's so sodding clever! What about the hit-man who was caught down in the cells with a shooter? Did he give you any idea who briefed him to waste me?'

'He's not said a word,' retorted the chief superintendent. 'He won't even give us his name or say where he lives. But when we'd scrubbed him down to the real man under his tramp's disguise, we reckoned he had to be a Yank. He wasn't known to any of the American Services over here, or to the Immigration and Aliens Department at the Home Office, so he had to be an illegal immigrant. We sent copies of his finger-prints by telex to the FBI at Washington and they identified him as a professional assassin called Junior. They want him back to face several murder charges, so we're going to extradite him. We haven't got much to charge him with here, apart from assaulting the police and carrying a firearm in a public place with intent to endanger life.'

'What about his attempted murder on me?' complained Garbutt in an aggrieved tone.

'Oh, but there's no proof of his intent towards you,' said Pritchard smoothly. 'He didn't shoot you, did he?'

'No, but he was about two seconds off, that's all.'

'Well, he refused to tell us who briefed him to kill you, so it's up to you to name your employer. Then we can maybe do something about it.'

'All right. His name's Blackstock.

Joseph Blackstock,' declared Garbutt vindictively. 'Do you know him?'

'Can't say I do. He's never come to the notice of the Robbery Squad.'

'Well, he bloody well should have done by now if you lot were on the ball. Big-time robbery is what he's into. He did the Dulwich bank security van last week, and I can name you the three others who were in it with us, as long as my name's left out.'

'That's understood of course,' Pritchard assured him.

'Blackstock did the silver-bullion robbery two years ago when the van was stopped and hijacked in the Blackwall Tunnel. I know. I was there. Then there was the raid on the Co-op Depot at Brentford where half a million was nicked.'

'That'll do for the moment,' said the chief superintendent, glancing at his sergeant who was scribbling rapidly in shorthand. 'I'd like a few of the finer details of those crimes you've mentioned before we go any farther.'

'You mean the other names? Sure, you can have 'em. I don't owe those bastards anything. And there's something else you can have as a bonus. Blackstock works with another cove, a sort of sleeping partner who gets him the information about these jobs to be hit. I heard it said he's a fat rich old bugger who lives up Hampstead, somebody called Mannion. But I've never seen him anywhere near the job. It's always Blackstock who gets us all together and draws up the plan and gives the orders. He's a bloody good leader who leads from in front and takes as much risk as anybody. I'll say that for him. And the way he thinks of everything and organises it down to the last detail, you lot wouldn't nab him in a hundred years without my help. So what about that pension to keep me out of trouble when I have to go and set up abroad? It's worth it to you, getting all those bastards off your back . . .'

★ ★ ★

As the days passed, Vic Mannion waited eagerly by the telephone to hear the message from Sam Junior, telling him that the long nightmare of Tom Garbutt, Supergrass, was over and he could return to his former carefree way of life. But the phone call never came. Nor was there any report in any newspaper of a prisoner having died in his cell.

In desperation Vic asked Reuben Levine if Tom Garbutt was still thriving in Walthamstow Police Station. The lawyer informed him with an oddly speculative look that Garbutt had been moved to Vine Street Police Station where he could be kept under closer guard and that he was visited regularly by Detective Chief Superintendent Pritchard of the Robbery Squad.

Vic could no longer delude himself. The potential Supergrass was alive and well, being wined and dined by the Top Brass of the Robbery Squad, seduced by their golden promises and singing his head off with all the fact and fiction he'd ever heard about Joe Blackstock and his shadowy business partner, Victor Mannion.

Whatever had happened to the doubly

recommended, high-performance hit-man, Vic would never know, but he'd taken six thousand quid of Vic's money down the drain with him and nothing had been solved.

13

Enjoying the long sunny days of his holiday in Paris, Joe Blackstock located the newspaper offices of *Le Figaro* just past the Rond Point at the bottom of the Champs Elysées. The vast front door of *Le Figaro*'s offices was close to the Franklin D. Roosevelt Metro Station. He walked up the marble stairs to the long mahogany reception desk, where a highly intellectual-looking receptionist told him that Monsieur Doumont was in his office and must not be disturbed. Would Monsieur care to leave a message to be passed on?

'No,' replied Joe. 'No message. But would you be kind enough to point out Monsieur Doumont to me when he comes out?'

Joe hung about near the desk, watching the frantic comings and goings at *Le Figaro*, and after about an hour he received a conspiratorial signal from the receptionist. She was indicating a tall dark man in his thirties, well built and fashionably dressed in Italian suit and shoes. With his dark hair and neatly trimmed Imperial beard and his similar physique, Alain Doumont bore a superficial resemblance to Joe Blackstock. But the Frenchman moved with nervous agitation in a state of highly strung tension and he chain-smoked his Gauloises as if his life depended on them.

Whatever her other shortcomings, Yvonne had good taste in men, thought Joe complacently as he took stock of the journalist.

'*Pardonnez-moi, M'sieur*,' said Joe in his passable French. 'You may be able to help me. I think we have a friend in common.'

'*Quoi*!' exclaimed Doumont in surprised irritation. 'What friend? I do not know you, and least of all your friends. Excuse me, M'sieur. I have an appointment.'

'Her name is Yvonne Belmondo,' persisted Joe. 'She said she's a friend of yours.'

Doumont flinched and stiffened with shock, his dark piercing eyes changing from suspicion to outright hostility.

'Why do you ask me about Yvonne Belmondo?'

'I'm trying to find her. It's rather urgent that I succeed. I thought you would know where she's likely to be staying in Paris.'

'I did not even know she was in Paris,' fumed the journalist. 'What causes you to believe I would know her whereabouts?'

'She's a great admirer of yours,' replied Joe blandly. 'She saves all your articles from *Le Figaro*. She told me she was your fiancée.'

'What!' spat Doumont venomously, bristling like a man confronted with a costly indiscretion which he is trying hard to forget. 'She told you that? *Sale putain! Je m'en fiche!*'

Waving his arms in violent dismissal he hurried away, puffing at his Gauloise like a runaway steamer, almost bursting with self-righteous rage.

Evidently, thought Joe wryly, Alain Doumont had discovered the truth about

151

Yvonne and found her a bloody nuisance, whatever their relationship had been at the start. Now his blood pressure shot up off the clock even at the mention of her name. But that didn't necessarily mean Yvonne had gone cold on him when she still saved his political bombast. She was probably still following him around with a bad case of unrequited love and sooner or later she would make contact.

So the following day Joe returned to the precincts of *Le Figaro* and waited outside the newspaper offices for Alain Doumont to emerge. He then followed him discreetly round and about Paris by Metro, autobus and taxi. An apéritif at the popular American Bar in the Champs Elysées; a lunch appointment at Lapérouse in the Quai des Grands Augustins, with a rotund, bearded, self-satisfied man wearing the ribbon of the Légion d'Honneur, obviously a politician on the gravy-train.

The following afternoon Doumont had an assignment at a tall elegant eighteenth-century house, still regal in its faded splendour, in the fashionable

Rue Mebillon near St. Germain des Près. Soon after Alain Doumont had been admitted to the house by a uniformed maid servant, Joe saw a handsome dark-haired woman showing a lot of cleavage appear momentarily at a first-floor window and deliberately close the shutters with an air of teasing, smouldering languor.

Much later in the afternoon Alain emerged looking tired and furtively triumphant. He was so relaxed that he didn't even light up one of his eternal Gauloises. Joe followed him home to the Latin Quarter where he lived picturesquely in a third-floor flat in a shabby old house in the Rue Tournefort. Joe checked with the concierge that Monsieur Doumont lived in Numéro Six.

It seemed all very regular, predictable and conventional, everything that a successful journalist's life should be. Alain was a busy, well integrated, well adjusted man, and he did not seem to have any room in his life for the hero-worshipping Yvonne. He'd nearly blown a gasket at the suggestion that he was her fiancé.

As the days slipped by without Yvonne putting in an appearance and Alain seemed to be managing his life very well without her, Joe began to fear he'd drawn the wrong conclusion. Even if Yvonne was in Paris she hadn't surfaced and couldn't have anything on the boil with the distinguished journalist on *Le Figaro*.

In fact Joe's initial deductions about them had been very close to the truth and Alain was now having trouble with Yvonne. He'd been studiously keeping out of her way for months. As far as Alain was concerned the torrid affair was over. It had burnt with too intense a heat to endure for long, but Yvonne expected it to last for ever.

They had met on one of Yvonne's trips to Paris with a charter flight and it had been love at first sight. After the gaucherie of Yvonne's initiation she had shown herself such an apt and ardent pupil that she had made even the blasé Alain think great things about the *Amour*. But then Alain, who was ambitious in the political and social arena, soon perceived that Yvonne was the kind of *cocotte* an intelligent man should never encourage as a permanent companion. She could so easily become a bore, an embarrassment and a liability. She did not have the kind of manners and refinement that a man of the world expects in his hostess wife, who should be the mainstay of his family life and the admiration of all those men in a position to advance his career.

Alain thought Yvonne was basically vulgar, grasping and not very intelligent. She didn't even know that the infallible way to put a man off for life is to chase him too abjectly. She was greedy and demanding; her tastes and ideals were petty bourgeois, and as for her temper, *Mon Dieu*! A man would feel awkward about presenting her to his professional friends and positively vulnerable at unveiling her to his enemies. To Alain respectability was back among the virtues and furthermore Yvonne could bring no settlement to a marriage. Definitely she was *une grande affaire* which should now have its inevitable ending.

Yvonne did not see things in that light. She was hounding the unfortunate Alain at a time when he'd found his true love, a woman whom he could look up to, the wife of a banker and a deputy, who shone with the glory of her aristocratic affluence. That glory now reflected on Alain and he felt he was worthy of the prestige which the love of Madeleine spread around him. He visited her lovely home three afternoons a week and made her happy in her perfumed boudoir, while her worthy, wealthy sexual turn-off of a husband was busy doing great things for France.

On the evening following Joe Blackstock's encounter with Alain Doumont, While Joe was off watch, enjoying his evening meal at a chic restaurant in the Place Clichy, Yvonne with her suitcase turned up at Alain's flat in the Latin Quarter and rang his doorbell.

'*Mon Dieu*!' He muttered, his face falling dejectedly. 'What are you doing here?'

156

'I couldn't wait to see you again, *chéri*,' she replied, planting a kiss on his coldly unresponsive lips. 'You do not seem very happy to see me, Alain. I remember you were keen enough to take me inside and have me stay the night when I first came here.'

'Oh, all right,' he retorted grudgingly. 'If it is a place to stay in Paris for one night, I do not refuse. I presume it is your business with the English airline that brings you here?'

As soon as she'd walked into his cosy, shabby sitting-room, put her suitcase down and poured herself a large Grand Marnier from his well-stocked drinks table, Yvonne disillusioned him.

'I have quit my job with the English charter company,' she stated calmly. 'I have come home to live permanently in Paris.'

'*Merde*! But why?'

'To be near you, darling. What else? Also you seem to forget that Paris is my real home. I am in exile away from it. I am, oh so sick of the dirty little bed-sit in London among the uncivilised *Anglais*,

157

and the cold-hearted, very hygienic Swiss in Basle. I want to come home.'

'You are running away from a man,' he said with sudden recollection, 'an Englishman.'

'So that is the story of my life,' she rejoined sadly. 'I run from all men, except you, Alain. You are the only man I want, and it is you who run away from me.'

He shrugged with callous indifference to her brimming tears.

'That is not my affair. We had our little *amour*, and outside the bed it does not work. So would you have me feeling guilt for ever? Please understand, Yvonne, I have my own life to lead. I can let you stay here the night, perhaps even two nights. But it would not be possible to have you here all the time. I must entertain my colleagues, converse with eminent men. I cannot be constantly hiding you under the bed when a distinuished executive of *Le Figaro* calls here to talk of affairs.'

'I understand,' replied Yvonne bitterly. 'You are ashamed of me now. But don't worry. I shall not embarrass you before your superior friends.'

'Thank you for that,' said Alain with obvious relief. 'How will you live now you are in Paris? The unemployment problem is very serious and it is getting worse now that the wretched socialists have won power.'

'Oh, I shall find some way of earning money,' she replied confidently. 'An air hostess has many skills. In any case there is no immediate crisis. I have my savings which will last for some weeks while I am looking around.'

As her eyes devoured him with sadness and longing, she wondered curiously how his attitude towards her would change if she now opened her suitcase before his astonished eyes and showed him the fortune she'd won in crisp new sterling bank-notes: a real *dot* with which to endow the man who loved her. But she resisted the temptation to buy Alain's love in such a crude, vulgar, humiliating way. Yvonne had her pride. Someday perhaps, if Alain ever proved worthy of her, she would surprise him at her own chosen moment, spring it on him in a time of shared rapture that she was now an heiress in her own right. She could buy him the carefree life of luxury and leisure that every civilised man secretly craved, even though he liked to boast that he was happy in his work. Then Alain would not be too proud to have her in his flat in case his intellectual friends from *Le Figaro* disapproved of her.

When they went to bed that night Alain wanted her to sleep on the unused spare bed in the guest-room. Yvonne was furious at the implied rejection and lack of gallantry. After all they'd been to each other and done together, he now obviously found her undesirable.

When she climbed naked into his bed and tried to rape him, his complete lack of interest, the apparent death of his virility pointed her to the obvious conclusion: his sex drive was all used up. He did not want Yvonne because he was getting plenty of fully satisfying sex elsewhere. Alain was not the man to be supine and flaccid before anything female unless he had absolute exhausting repletion very often. He must have another mistress who kept him fulfilled and happy! Yvonne fairly bristled with venomous, despairing rage at the prospect.

She leapt out of his bed and stormed into the kitchen where she filled a large water-jug with ice-cold water. As Alain lay on his back naked, dozing fitfully from sheer exhaustion after his recent strenuous bout of pure love with la belle Madeleine, Yvonne ripped the duvet off him and poured the four litres of cold water all over his torpid and useless organ.

Alain leapt up with a violent yell of rage and a long tirade of foul obscenities. He chased her round the flat, grabbed her and beat her savagely. He slapped her face first with the open palm of his hand and then with the back of it, until her head rang like a gong and she was partially stunned. But Yvonne didn't care. She laughed and sobbed and clung to him hysterically. Even this kind of emotional attention from her man was better than the cold indifference she'd met so far.

When he'd beaten her to her knees he

twisted her arm up behind her back and hustled her out of the flat on to the dimly lit landing. Then he threw all her clothes and her precious suitcase out after her, slammed the door, locked and bolted it and adjusted the security chain with the harsh clash of finality.

Ah, that suitcase! If only he knew! thought Yvonne despairingly as she struggled into her clothes and went weeping down the stairs to find somewhere to stay for the rest of the night.

The following day she took a room in a small cheap *pension* near the Porte d'Italie and lived modestly out of her suitcase, changing the sterling as she needed it at a nearby bank, pretending to be an English student. She kept her jackpot in the suitcase under her bed and changed only a small sum at a time to cover her current needs. She was cunning enough to know the folly of splashing it around ostentatiously and attracting attention. Allowing its existence to become known was how the so-clever Monsieur Blackstock had succeeded in losing it.

Meanwhile Yvonne had an obsessive, raging, single-minded purpose of finding out the identity of her rival, the *putain* who had taken Alain away from her, and if possible of doing her a mischief. For Yvonne was a fighter who would always fight like a tigress for what she really wanted. She would never accept the freeze-off from the only man she'd ever loved.

She hired a car and began furtively to follow Alain round Paris on his daily news-seeking errands and extra professional activity, from his home in the Rue Tournefort to the offices of *Le Figaro* and thence to his devotions with his new mistress in that haughty other world just off St. Germain des Près.

14

Having discovered where Alain met his mistress, Yvonne found it equally easy to nose round and ascertain who she was: the loaded, idolised, pampered young wife of a wealthy banker and member of the Chamber of Deputies, Monsieur Jean Michel de Lassigny.

Yvonne was too intimidated by Madeleine's imposing façade of wealth and grandeur of living to walk in and assault her and scratch her eyes out, as female honour demanded. But one sure way she believed she could hurt her hated rival was to tip off the unsuspecting husband as to what his devoted little wife got up to with a disreputable journalist three afternoons a week.

Yvonne started sending lurid sexually scurrilous anonymous letters to the doting husband at his business address on the Boulevard Haussman. She told him Alain's identity and profession, his home address, the usual time of the assignation and sundry obscene intimate details of Alain's speciality, dredged up from her own remembered experiences.

She didn't know precisely how she could ever hope to recapture Alain's affection by this naive and gutter-style exposing of the guilty lovers. But she had some muddled idea that by bringing down some kind of retribution on those two copulating animals who greedily took their own pleasure and shut Yvonne right out, she might succeed in destroying Alain's attachment to Madeleine.

It was while she was torturing herself, following Alain assiduously all over Paris in order to assure herself that he had no other mistresses for her to get rid of that Yvonne chanced to see Joe Blackstock. He hadn't seen her, for her diminutive figure in the crowd gave her the advantage. She was being jostled and racketed around on the Metro, her dumpy figure submerged and squashed between other standing passengers in the crowded carriage next to Alain's, when she spotted the tall figure and unmistakable profile of Joe Blackstock, similarly employed in following the magnetic Alain.

Yvonne nearly curled up on the spot and died with fright. If Blackstock was in Paris it could only be in pursuit of her and the stolen money. How could he have found out that she'd come to Paris? It was an unbelievable disaster. She felt sick and chilled with the breath of doom. In Yvonne's world women were never in any doubt of the kind of treatment reserved for them by the men they cheated and betrayed. When Blackstock caught up with her he would probably disfigure her for life, slash her face with a razor, and knock all her teeth out, or possibly dream up something even worse.

She fought her way out of the carriage at the next stop and, still obscured from Blackstock by the tidal deluge of humanity, hurried upwards out into the street. Blackstock hadn't spotted her. She was sure of that. It was a fantastic piece of luck that she'd managed to see him first. She took a taxi home to her *pension* and shut herself in her room for the rest of the day, shivering with terror. She didn't dare go out for her midday meal to the little *routiers'* brasserie on the corner in case Joe Blackstock should chance to call in there. What was she going to do? If Blackstock once found out where she was living, the least she could expect was that he would take back all her lovely money, even if he left her physically intact.

Yvonne couldn't bear the thought of that bereavement. Her inexhaustible supply of money was now an essential condition of her life. She would be naked, helpless and lost without it. The fear of its loss was a permanent waking nightmare. Above all, her money was the one sure guarantee that she would eventually be able to buy back Alain's love for herself. He obviously had no future with Madeleine de Lassigny who would never leave her rich home, her friends and social milieu for a penniless journalist. Alain would one day need a practical and loyal wife with a handsome *dot* and that was when Yvonne would come into her own.

The immediate appalling danger to all that was Joe Blackstock. With him rampaging round Paris like a killer shark to recover the money he'd lost, Yvonne had to have her fortune securely hidden, far away from her *pension* room which Blackstock would turn upside down once he'd located her. She had the peasant's distrust of banks, especially where hot money in a foreign currency was concerned. She dared not leave her suitcase in her mother's small flat out in the suburbs. The old woman was nosy, avaricious and spendthrift. Once she discovered all that money in the suitcase she would get her greedy hands in it, drinking, gambling, buying gimcrack rubbish and fancy hats until there was nothing left. There was no other place to hide the suitcase but in Alain's flat. She knew he had a fair-sized lumber-room next to the kitchen, filled with old crates, broken picture frames, disused furniture and other household junk which one hoards automatically when one is too much a hoarding squirrel to throw useless things away.

Alain hardly ever looked inside his lumber-room except occasionally to dump some other household item which he'd renewed. Yvonne could hide her money there and Alain would never dream he was her banker until she chose to enlighten him. Blackstock would never find it in a thousand years, for how could he know about her close association with Alain Doumont?

Yvonne still had her duplicate key to Alain's flat, which he'd had specially cut for her, a survival from the days when they were passionate lovers and he was only too glad to come home from the office to find Yvonne waiting there with his slippers, a well prepared meal and her ever welcoming loving arms.

She waited until mid-afternoon when she knew Alain was safely preoccupied with his obscene carryings-on in the Rue Mebillon. Having taken from the suitcase a couple of thousand pounds for immediate expenses, which she concealed in her capacious handbag and about her person, she took the rest of her precious hoard by taxi over to Alain's flat in the

Latin Quarter. She looked constantly over her shoulder for the dreaded sight of Joe Blackstock, but he was nowhere around.

Yvonne had long been on nodding terms with the concierge in the tall old house where Alain lived, so the old woman thought nothing of her comings and goings. She hardly noticed Yvonne with her white suitcase arrive there and walk nonchalantly up the three gloomy flights of stairs to the flat of such happy memories. Yvonne let herself in and walked through the suspended dust-motes in the shuttered, silent rooms.

It was a spacious, rambling, homely flat, full of old fashioned furniture, with the carpets and decorations in that dingy twilight condition that in Paris creates the unforgettable atmosphere. Each heavy piece of rosewood and battered gilt was redolent of Alain in all his glory and breathed the fading opulence of a more fortunate epoch. The wide old-fashioned brass bedstead, big enough to accommodate two loving couples in simultaneous productivity, where she had surrendered her virginity to Alain, still dominated the spacious bedroom with its view over the rooftops of Montmartre and Sacré Coeur. She stood looking round for some moments with fond, tearfilled eyes, wishing herself back in the first night of love when Alain had murmured such wonderful things in her ear. Then resolutely she turned away to the kitchen and the adjoining lumber-room.

Picking her way over dusty boxes, broken piss-pots and battered picture frames, she penetrated to the darkest corner of the junk-room and there deposited her treasure under a decrepit old table with two broken legs. She spread some moth-eaten curtains over it to complete the interment and then quietly withdrew, feeling secure and well satisfied with the arrangement.

15

The husband of Alain's expensive mistress
was not a man to cuckold light-
heartedly. A right-wing politician, former
Colonel of the paratroops in the French
Army in Algeria, he was still at heart
a passionate supporter of the Algérie
Française movement all these years after
the issue was dead and buried. He had
played a considerable part behind the
scenes in the Generals' Revolt over
Algeria twenty years ago. He had never
forgiven Big Charlie for the sellout to
the *fellaghas*, the severing of the trunk of
Metropolitan France and the betrayal of
his country's honour. Though he was too
well known now to those who mattered
in Paris to associate openly with the small
surviving clique of O.A.S. plotters, he
wasn't above contributing anonymously
to the funds of those altruistic patriots
who occasionally left plastic bombs and
the dead bodies of political enemies

around for the Honour of France.

For years Colonel de Lassigny had been a sincere well-wisher of those who had a mission to liquidate the President. But having seen several well planned attempts to rub out Big Charlie fail ignominiously and bring down rigorous punishment on those responsible, he'd resigned himself to the second-rate status quo and consoled himself by making money.

When De Gaulle was dead and also forgotten, the vendetta seemed to lose its point, even though de Lassigny would have liked to dig up Charles de Gaulle from his shrine at Colombey-les-Deux-Eglises and kill him all over again. But the colonel got married instead to an heiress and made even more money.

Colonel Jean Michel de Lassigny, Croix de Guerre, Légion d'Honneur, was a gross formidable man in his late fifties. He was short and stockily built with thinning grizzled hair, a thick hooked nose, mobile piercing eyes and a brick-red complexion that owed its colour as much to good living as to its long years

173

in the Algerian sun. He always wore the ribbon of the Légion d'Honnuer on the lapel of his dark blue pin-striped suit so that nobody could ever forget he'd earned it. By birth an aristocrat, by conviction a French patriot, by accomplishment a distinguished soldier and a businessman, by destiny a cuckold, he wasn't a man who boiled his cabbages twice and he had surrounded himself with efficiency.

From his spacious suite of offices on the Boulevard Haussman, looking out over the majestic scene to the Place de la Concorde, de Lassigny was painfully hatching a brew of murderous rage as he read yet another of the scurrilous anonymous letters he'd started getting about his wife's *amours* under his own roof with some nasty little journalist.

The colonel was a man of the world. He didn't really give a damn how Madeleine occupied her spare time. Every woman had to have a hobby. She was thirty and he was nearly sixty and there would have been something sadly wrong with her if she hadn't got a virile young lover or two tucked away somewhere for her pleasure. But he thought at least she was well bred enough to be discreet about it, not to besmirch her husband's name and honour by letting her squalid affaires become public property.

Any day now this piece of *merde* who'd somehow got to know of Madeleine's antics would be approaching him for money to keep it quiet. And if he didn't pay up with a good grace, the news of his dishonour would be spread all over Paris. It would be slyly and obliquely hinted at in the prestigious gossip columns. All Paris society would be laughing at him in their sleeves, for even in this permissive and immoral age the cuckolding of eminent and valiant men was still a source of prime amusement, even to blasé, civilised Parisians.

By God, it was not to be endured!

Apart from all the shame, ridicule and petty malice, he just couldn't afford financially to risk losing Madeleine to some worthless adventurer. Madeleine came from a powerful family and had money in her own right [the reason why he'd given her his name] and it

175

had bought her a substantial holding in her husband's merchant bank. Judging by what was going on according to these filthy letters, her affair with that gutter rat must be something more serious than the usual married woman's roll in the hay. Supposing she wanted to go away with her lover and leave the colonel altogether! That would mean she would want to pull her money out of her investment. Passionate elopements always need a cold financial backing. And this at a time when the leech-like socialists under that *voyou* Mitterand had their sticky hands in all the colonel's pockets! This at a time when he needed all his liquid reserves to finance a big new project with Sud Aviation! If the House de Lassigny should be financially embarrassed or even tainted with the slightest uncertainty at a time like this, it would be a shattering disaster. It could even touch off a new panic on the Bourse. A wave of selling! My God! The mere thought of it almost gave him a heart condition.

Patriotic considerations alone and high affairs of state demanded that this miserable Alain Doumont should be removed from the scene abruptly, since he had the execrable taste to meddle with things the far-ranging repercussions of which he knew nothing and could know nothing.

Colonel de Lassigny prided himself on being first and foremost a soldier. Therefore he liked playing soldiers with all aspects of life and making big, irrevocable, soldierly decisions with brisk alacrity. He picked up the telephone on his desk and dialled the number of a shabby shoemaker's shop in the narrow, cobbled Rue Domat in the oldest and sleaziest part of the Latin Quarter. Above the shop in a low-roofed mansard room a former O.A.S. gunman known as René Bruard — René le Sceau to his peers — ex-paratrooper, pimp, thief and commercial assassin, lived, loved and brawled in sultry squalor with his favourite prostitute.

The colonel arranged to meet him at noon in a club just off the Champs Elyeées known as Le Sexy. Here over a glass of fine old brandy, in a furtive, cloak and dagger tête-à-tête, the outraged colonel pronounced sentence of death on one Alain Doumont, distinguished man of affairs, political correspondent of *Le Figaro* and *persona non grata* to elderly husbands with flighty, sex-crazy young wives.

René Bruard was a tough, stocky, illiterate man of forty-five with oily skin and black bristly hair which he wore crew cut in the American fashion. His main distinguishing feature was a hideous lurid scar from temple to jawbone, where the knife slash of a fellagha in the Souk at Algiers had laid it open. René had served for six years as an N.C.O. in the Paratroops in Algeria and was a spiritual casualty of that brutal war. Having gone the whole hog with the fellaghas, having seen the mutilated bodies of his comrades with their balls cut off and stuffed in their mouths, he was not disposed to be squeamish about anything. He found it just a well paid, run-of-the-mill assignment to pull the trigger on some nonentity who was imbecile enough to monkey about with the woman of a colonel in the Paras.

In dealing with this man from his old battalion who would be faithful to him to the death, de Lassigny adopted the tone of peremptory commanding officer and benevolent monarch.

'I will give you a hundred thousand francs,' he said ferociously, 'half now, and the other half when I shall have read Doumont's obituary in *Le Figaro*.'

'*Bien, mon Colonel. D'accord*,' nodded René approvingly.

'And you must arrange a little holiday for your health immediately afterwards,' ordered the colonel grimly. 'Go to Spain or Italy or Morocco for a month or two. In Algiers of course you would not be welcome. If the police should be looking for a professional assassin after the death of Dourmont, it would be good for you not to be here. They already know that you served in my battalion in Algeria, and if they look for reasons why I would want him dead, perhaps they would not have to search very far, with gossip in high society being what it is.'

'That is true, *mon Colonel*.'

179

'Do not communicate with me, and do not try to meet me from henceforth. I will make all the arrangements for paying you what I owe as soon as I shall have read Doumont's death announcement in the newspapers. Have you understood?'

'*Compris, mon Colonel*,' grunted René, stuffing the thick wad of bank-notes into his breast pocket.

He stood up, snapped stiffly to attention and saluted respectfully, for with his long-ingrained discipline he still saw this bloated plutocrat in civilian dress as endowed with all the authority and charisma of the French Army.

'You are sure you can find Doumont without mistakes?'

'Yes, my Colonel. I have his address.'

16

Yvonne had been keeping to her room in the *pension* and only venturing out like a wanted criminal to the nearby shops to buy necessities. She had thus avoided being seen by Joe Blackstock and he was even more resigned to the fact that his smart deduction about Alain Doumont's being Yvonne's lover had been wrong. In all probability he had lost Yvonne, who was living it up on his money in some other European playground. However, he was enjoying his holiday in Paris and was in no hurry to move on. He knew he would catch up with that thieving slut this year, next year or the year after. He counted time like an oriental when it was a question of paying off a grudge.

Yvonne had probably gone south for the winter and he decided to spend some time in Rome looking for her there.

In the meantime he continued his surveillance on Alain Doumont. He followed him daily about Paris, picking him up outside the office of *Le Figaro*, or emerging from the arms of his fashionable mistress, or coming from the tall apartment building where he lived in the Rue Tournefort. Joe was increasingly interested in the strange assortment of people and places that the journalist was familiar with. It was an entirely new Paris that the foreigner and the tourist hardly ever saw.

Eventually Yvonne became bored and restless with being alone all day in the chilly inhospitable room of the *pension*. She longed for a sight of Alain, even though he was rude and impatient with her and would quickly brush her off. She had to know where he was and what he was still doing, even though it was a diabolical torment to follow him to the home of his wealthy mistress and watch her closing the shutters on the whole world.

Yvonne rebelled against discretion. Suddenly she realised how much she wanted Alain all to herself, away from this cold heartless Paris which was now fraught with such terrible danger for her. To hide from the streets like an animal and look for her hunter round every corner was becoming a nerve-racking ordeal. Boldly she resolved to persuade Alain to leave Paris with her, even though she had to risk playing her last trump card and tell him about the cash fortune in her suitcase.

She bolstered up her courage and began to follow Alain again. To hell with Blackstock anyway! Paris was a big place to find one person in and whatever happened her money was safe from his thieving hands.

In a street off the Rue Pierre Charron that cuts across the Avenue Georges Cinq before reaching the Champs Elysées, Alain stopped at a shabby bistro with a toothpaste striped awning over the pavement and its frontage plastered with Dubonnet and Lager labels. Alain was a creature of routine and he always went to that particular bistro for his mid-morning glass of wine and a snack and a leisurely look at his own daily article in newsprint.

Yvonne went up to him humbly and sat down at the same table in the almost empty bistro. Alain looked up from *Le Figaro* with narrowed eyes, gave a snort of disapproval on recognising her and then lit up a Gauloise, blowing the acrid smoke unchivalrously into her face.

'*Merde alors!* You again?' he said icily. 'Are you ineducable? Did you deduce nothing when I flung you out the other night?'

'Please don't be angry with me. Alain,' she began, turning her adoring eyes on him. 'I just wanted to see you for a few minutes.'

'Yes, yes,' he answered irritably. '*Comment ça va?*'

'Alain, I need your help. I am in terrible trouble. Please take me away from Paris.'

Sacré bleu! Was the woman mad?

He stared at her unbelievingly and then laughed in her face unpleasantly.

'Oh yes, that would be magnificent! For you who ruin my bed with water in gratitude, I am supposed to sacrifice my whole life! Even if I were mad enough to run away with you, how shall I do my work away from Paris when I must work on a French newspaper? How shall I live? Tell me that, you who are so full of wonderful ideas.'

'When you first seduced me you swore that you loved me,' she cried accusingly.

He made an obscene gesture which disowned her innocence completely, and began to refold his newspaper.

'I must go now. I have an appointment. If you want to leave Paris, that is fine. But you will go alone as far as I am concerned.'

'Please, *cher* Alain, don't leave me,' she cried desperately. 'I have more to tell you, something very important. You do not have to worry any more about working for money. I have enough for us both, for the rest of our lives.'

Alain froze in mid-gesture and slumped back in his chair as if somebody had winded him.

'What was that you just said, Yvonne? How much money? How much is enough for us both for the rest of our lives? Tell me what you mean, Yvonne.'

She started to tell him of the big money robbery of a bank security van in Dulwich, London on September 3rd, when bandits had escaped with two hundred thousand pounds.

He interrupted impatiently.

'*Merde!* Those decadent, immoral English are always committing great robberies. They stole even the World Cup of Association Football some years ago, I remember: the Ark of the Covenant of their dreary God, Sport. So what have you to do with a commonplace English bank robbery, Yvonne?'

She plunged on recklessly, telling how the arch-villain who'd planned the robbery, Joe Blackstock, was a close friend of the captain of her aircraft, another typical English crook called Rowland Seaton. Blackstock had come aboard the aircraft carrying a suitcase full of money, which he dare not risk taking past the customs officers, and which he intended to bank in Switzerland. She explained in detail how she had managed to get the suitcase away from him while he was busily defending himself against the other

186

crooks she had hired to help her. And now she had the money safe in her suitcase nearly a hundred thousand pounds, all for herself and Alain.'

He stared at her open-mouthed with admiration and delight. He suddenly remembered the tall *Anglais* who'd accosted him at *Le Figaro*'s office, asking him if he knew the whereabouts of Yvonne Belmonde because it was very urgent. It all fitted neatly into the pattern to confirm the truth of Yvonne's story.

Suddenly this girl Yvonne had taken on a strange and remarkable beauty. He had never stopped to consider before what a wonderful smile she had, how practical she was about the house, how loyal and steadfast towards him. And in the bed she was *magnifique*! He could certainly vouch for that. What a desirable, wholesome wife for a staunch catholic who, under French law, would automatically become the custodian of her worldly goods!

'Bravo, *mon petit chou*!' he crowed. 'You are a miracle. You are wonderful for the morale. How much did you say, one hundred thousand pounds sterling? That is — ' He did a rapid mental calculation — 'well over a million francs! But Yvonne, it is a fortune. One could buy a vineyard on the Loire, a villa in Monaco, a little hostel in Provence. One could abandon the struggle and the toil and become at last truly civilised. Newspapers! *Merde* to all newspapers! The way I have to fight to stay alive in this Paris and satisfy those slave-owning newspaper proprietors, I shall have two ulcers before I am forty. My little cabbage, you have saved my life!'

Yvonne was too besotted by him not to be deeply moved and flattered by his sudden access of tender admiration for her. If she suspected deep in her crafty little soul that it was only her money he'd fallen violently in love with, she resolutely suppressed the nasty thought.

'*Chéri*, you will take me away from Paris where I am so much in danger?'

'But of course, *petit chou*.'

'Today? At once?'

Alain became cagey as he paused for some rapid thinking to take stock of the new situation. He wasn't going to be driven anywhere precipitately by a woman, even though she did possess a million francs. Yvonne with the money was good. The money without Yvonne would be even better. But the money with Madeleine to sweeten it and make it sing would be absolute delirium.

'I have arrangements to make before I can go, some tidying up to do,' he said warily. 'One does not flee to the south every day of one's life. I cannot just quit *Le Figaro* with a '*je m'en fiche*!' Things must be honourably wound up to such a career. Give me a week to settle everything and make my exit.'

'But Alain,' she cried desperately, 'I am afraid for my life. I dare not stay in Paris a day longer. That evil Monsieur Blackstock, the great robber is here looking for me. I have seen him on the Metro. Any moment he might find me, and then I shall be kaput. He will take all the money away from us, and perhaps cut my throat for stealing it from him.'

'In that case you must stay all the time in your room, in your *pension*,' said Alain urgently. 'Do not go out even into the street. I will bring you food and magazines to read until we are both ready to leave Paris.'

'But I shall go mad,' cried Yvonne plaintively. 'You don't know what it is like to stay shut up in that dreary place all day and every day. I have had enough of living in fear. I want to leave Paris today to be with you.'

'Pouf! You make such a big trouble about nothing. In that case go on your own to the south. Write and tell me where you will be staying, and I will follow you there as soon as my business here is completed.'

'Alain,' she said hesitantly, 'there is something else you ought to know. There may be trouble for you also if you stay any longer in Paris.'

'What!'

He looked at her with a sudden cold incredulity and suspicion.

'What do you mean, Yvonne? How may there be trouble for me?'

'It is something that I did on the spur of the moment, without giving it proper thought. Please don't be angry with me, Alain. I did it only because I love you.'

'And what was it you did because you love me, my little cabbage?' said Alain in a dangerously civilised voice.

'I found out about your new friend, Madeleine de Lassigny in the Rue Mebillon. I found out who her husband is. I wrote a letter to Monsieur de Lassigny at his offices in the Boulevarde Haussman, telling him how you visit his wife in his house in the afternoons.'

'You did what?'

Alain went cold with rage and colder still with fear. He lashed Yvonne viciously across the face with a back-hander. It knocked her clean off her chair and sent her sprawling underneath the next table down among the evil-smelling spittoons.

The pot-bellied bistro proprietor behind his zinc-topped counter shrugged his shoulders up to his ears, made a typical French grimace of tolerant amusement and went on munching his croissant. It must be wonderful still to care so much about the *Amour*!

Yvonne picked herself up painfully,

shedding tears of contrition rather than resentment.

'Forgive me, Alain. I only wanted what is best for you. That woman, she is no good for an honest man like you. She would never leave her rich husband to be with you. You are only a bit of amusement for her. When she becomes bored she will leave you and break your heart.'

Alain hardly heard her. He was doing some rapid, panicstricken thinking. With Madeleine's husband out for his blood, it was definitely time to blow town. On the journalistic grapevine he had heard sinister rumours about Colonel de Lassigny and his former O.A.S. connections, some of whom probably still survived. They gave the colonel a fearful reputation for potential violence. Human life was cheaper than dirt to men like him. The most diabolical savagery was nothing compared with such a man's imagined dishonour. His chauvinistic arrogance, his strutting self-adulation, would never allow a humbler man like Alain Doumont to give him the horns and get away with it.

Men like Jean Michel de Lassigny still had the power of feudal despots through their money to make their enemies meet with fatal accidents.

'We will go today, *petit chou*,' he muttered, glancing at his watch. 'It is now 11.35. The *Mistral Rapide* leaves from the Gare de Lyon at approximately 17.30 for the Cote d'Azur. Meet me at the *guichet* of the Gare de Lyon no later than 17.10.'

'Oh, Alain,' she sobbed joyfully, 'we will be so happy just you and I. We will have a vineyard near Bordeaux and our own wine-cellar as you always dreamed, and dozens of children.'

'But of course, little one. Where did you say you had so cleverly hidden this famous suitcase with all the English money?' said Alain fondly, the admiration in his voice obscuring the eager curiosity. 'It would not of course be safe to leave it in your *pension* room.'

'It is safe in your lumber-room, *cheri*, next to the kitchen,' she confessed ingenuously.

'*Mon Dieu!*'

Alain nearly shot backwards off his chair. To be living so intimately with such an amount of money was a truly overwhelming experience when it first broke over one, like free-falling by parachute or inhaling champagne bubbles, or having one's first woman at thirteen.

'I knew you wouldn't mind,' she said eagerly. 'That was the only place I could think of that was completely safe from the English bandit. When I knew Blackstock was in Paris I was so afraid, and he would never dream of looking in your flat as he does not know you and I are together.'

'That was a very good thought,' said Alain admiringly.

'You are a very clever girl, Yvonne. I shall be getting a wonderful bargain in the marriage to you.'

'Oh, Alain, I am so happy!'

★ ★ ★

Out in the street Joe Blackstock strolled in leisurely fashion towards the bistro. It was one of Alain's regular ports of call each morning. Joe had seen him go there two or three times, and he knew his quarry, a creature of routine, would be inside there now enjoying his mid-morning refreshment.

As Joe glanced casually through the dirty cluttered window into the gloomy interior he saw the bistro was empty apart from the fat proprietor at his counter and two people sitting at a table. When he looked harder and recognised Yvonne Belmondo there in the flesh in cosy conversation with Alain, he blasphemed softly with incredulous triumph. Then he felt ten feet tall with a fierce soaring elation. It was that lousy thieving slut sure enough. His hunch had been right after all. At last the elusive animal had shown itself. Yvonne was no genius in the world of villainy. His own bad mismanagement and the other half of the money were about to be retrieved.

He walked round the corner and waited in a doorway with the bistro in view. Presently Alain and Yvonne came hurrying out and bustled off down the street arm in arm, chattering delightedly together like two lovers who had just found each other. Anyone could tell at a glance they were making idyllic plans for a lovely unclouded future on Joe's money. *Tout le monde* knows that a million francs, properly invested and put to work, will last for ever.

Joe followed them cautiously at a safe distance as far as the Place Blanche with the Place Clichy on the left and the Place Pigalle on the right, where the drugged and drunken drop-outs, the ponces, pushers and porn merchants slopped about the place as if they owned it. Alain and Yvonne parted here with a passionate kiss. *A Bientôt*! That night they would be having it off on wheels in a *Wagon Lit* and the spirit of Madeleine would be finally exorcised.

Alain went off to make what he called some essential last-minute arrangements for departure. Yvonne took an autobus to the Rue St. Michel to finalise her honeymoon shopping. Joe Blackstock followed her autobus in a taxi.

17

As soon as Yvonne was safely out of the way, Alain rushed into a kiosk, searched his pockets frantically for a jeton and then dialled Madeleine's number at her home in the Rue Mebillon. He blurted out his news as if he hadn't a minute to live.

'Madeleine, *chérie*, an emergency! I must leave Paris at once, *mon ange*. Your husband has found out everything.'

Madeleine laughed her soft, delightful, slightly throaty laugh which always made the hairs bristle ecstatically on Alain's belly.

'You sound frightened, my dear Alain. What is so suddenly wrong? You always knew I had a husband when you first coaxed me into an *affaire*, did you not? All husbands find out in the end. Those are the rules by which we play. It increases their feeling of insecurity, which can only work to our advantage in the long run.'

Alain was astounded at her flippant lack of fear for the sinister ex-colonel of paratroops whose ménage she shared.

'Perhaps you feel safe enough!' he shouted. 'I certainly do not! Your husband is an evil man who will want revenge for being given the horns. I must leave for the south today, lest I shall be hit by a speeding car or have weed-killer mixed with my coffee, or a booby-trapped bomb rigged up behind my door. Madeleine, *chérie*, come with me into the sun and share my life.'

'Must you really run away, little mouse? sighed Madeleine regretfully, with a subtle mélange of disappointment and mockery in her voice. 'Are you really so sensitive that you dare not face an old man nearly twice your age?'

'Madeleine, my darling, I am so sick of sharing you with him! I want you entirely for myself. Come with me today and we will make a new life together somewhere in the south.'

'I am very flattered by your offer,' said Madeleine soothingly, 'but I am bored with the south. I have spent the whole of August there, unable to escape from the vulgar tourists and foreigners who are everywhere. Now is the time to be in Paris where one is spiritually alive.'

'But I have money now,' cried Alain, becoming more and more excited. 'I have more than a million francs. I will take you anywhere you want to be.'

'Oh, that,' said Madeleine with a hint of distaste. 'I am sure you will know how to have fun with it, while it lasts. As for me, I want to be in Paris among my friends, going to parties, being civilised, being hostess for my husband's distinguished guests.'

'Then you do not love me enough? You will not come?' he cried with tears of grief and rage.

'It is quite out of the question, *mon cher*. I am preparing a *soirée* for some members of the *Académie française*. One has to supervise one's caterers so carefully these days. *Au revoir*, my little mouse, or is it to be *Adieu*? Be careful not to offend any husbands in the south. Call me when you will have returned to Paris with your courage. It is possible I may still be available.'

He heard her soft mocking laughter again and then the click as she hung up. Alain slammed down the receiver and rushed out of the kiosk like a man demented, furiously cursing all women to hell. Henceforth he would live only for himself. Yvonne's gift of great wealth had opened up a new vista of freedom and lack of care. Now he could really afford to be amoral. Devil take this cold, winter-bound northern capital where all men were beasts to one another, scratching backs one minute, tearing out throats the next. His hot blood yearned for the south, where he could live like a lotus-eater and drink life to the lees.

The frightening knowledge that the cuckolded husband had found out about his take-over, that he, Alain Doumont, might well incur the hired physical vengeance of that fanatical fascist reactionary acted on him like a rocket booster.

He rushed home and nearly flattened the concierge when she pottered out of her den in alarm to see who was in such a tearing hurry. He charged up the dark stairs three at a time to hurl himself into the musty gloom of his flat. He didn't even stop to open the shutters and let in the sunlight, but hurtled like a tornado into the lumber-room. Broken chairs, picture frames, piss-pots and water-jugs flew in all directions in a cloud of dust and shards as he hunted frenziedly for Yvonne's hidden treasure.

At last he found the white suitcase up the far corner covered by the moth-eaten curtains. He recognised it instantly as the one Yvonne had been carrying on that evening when she first came to his flat two weeks ago. The suitcase was locked and Yvonne had the key. He had no time to break it open, but accepted Yvonne's word for it that it contained the right stuff. He threw his passport, spare cash, credit cards, cheque-book and the best of his clothes into his own suitcase. Then he sat down hurriedly at his desk and wrote a formal letter of resignation as from that day to the Editor of *Le Figaro*. He explained that the sudden recrudescence of a deep-seated illness made his continuance as a journalist impossible. For his health's sake he had to leave Paris at once for a more equable climate. He addressed the envelope, sealed and stamped it and rushed on his way, mailing the letter at the first mailbox he came to.

Half an hour later he was at the Gare de Lyon buying a ticket for Marseilles. At 13.30 hours he was on the Mistral express, roaring through the southern suburbs of Paris at increasing speed on the long haul to a kinder environment and a fuller life.

Yvonne, he reflected callously, would deepen her knowledge of human nature and the ways of the world a little further when she arrived at the Gare de Lyon for their loving rendezvous in four hours' time and realised she'd been taken to the cleaners.

18

Yvonne went to an expensive restaurant on the Rue de Rivoli and really spread herself on what was to be the last meal she would eat in Paris for a long time. At length she decided to do her shopping in the Champs Elysées for her glamorous new honeymoon trousseau with which she was really going to electrify Alain when she got him all to herself in that *Wagon Lit*.

Joe Blackstock kept her patiently in sight and she was so engrossed in her window-shopping, choosing, bargaining, haggling and purchasing that she never once looked round to see Destiny on her tail. A saucy black bra and tiny black frilly gossamer pants no broader than a strip of ribbon seemed a good combination to get Alain's sap rising in the train. She had temporarily forgotten all about the menace of Joe Blackstock in the excitement of her pre-nuptial euphoria.

Yvonne arrived back at her *pension* feeling almost disembodied with joy, floating in a rose-coloured haze which was bearing her along to a wonderful fulfilment. No sooner had she got into her room, put down her parcels, taken off her coat and flashed her teeth admiringly at herself in the mirror on her dressing-table than she heard the door of her room open. She wheeled round with an exclamation of annoyance which was constricted in her throat in a croak of fear as she recognised the tall, well dressed, well groomed figure who sauntered into the room and kicked the door shut behind him.

'Hullo, Yvonne,' said Joe Blackshot. 'I've been longing to see you. I trailed you right across Europe in the course of our great romance.'

Yvonne just stared at him, pale to the lips, wide-eyed with horror.

'What do you want?' she finally muttered.

'That's a bloody daft question, all things considered. I want the suitcase you stole from me in Switzerland, and I hope for your sake you haven't gone through too much of my money, you stinking trash!'

'Trash yourself!' she retorted defiantly. 'You stole the money in the first place, so it doesn't belong to you. I have as much right to it as you have; more right, because I have it in my possession.'

'Don't let's waste time splitting hairs about title of ownership,' said Joe. 'The point is I organised and fought for that money. I risked a fifteen-year stretch in prison or worse. It was something more than just stealing to snatch it in the middle of Dulwich in broad daylight from men who were trained and qualified to defend it. I nearly got my face bashed in with a truncheon and I had to squirt ammonia in the eyes of some poor bastard. I reckon I earned that money ten times over. And what did you do to establish any claim to it, except creep along like a rat in a sewer to grab it and run, while I was preoccupied with the hoodlums you'd conned into doing your dirty work. So where's my money, you stinking dog-shit?'

'Piss off!' she spat malevolently. '*Fichez*

le camp, you animal!'

'Come, come,' said Joe with dangerous tolerance. 'You can do better than that. I know from past enlightenment that your foul vocabulary is equal to your squalid life pattern. I've spent nearly a fortnight in Paris trying to find you. I can spend another fortnight if I have to, beating the truth out of you. You'll tell me where it is in the end, so why not do yourself a favour? Relax and take the easy way out. Don't cause me any more trouble, and then I might leave you with your miserable life.'

'Don't dare to touch me!' she screamed. 'I'll call the flics and tell them you are a bank robber.'

'You know well enough criminals don't appeal to the police to get them off the hook,' said Joe. 'We execute our own impartial justice, lacking in polish though it may be. Go ahead and scream. Nobody would hear you, or bother much if they did. You wouldn't be the first little tart to yell her head off in vain in a French *pension*. Where's my suitcase and the money that you haven't spent?'

'*Foutez!*' she screamed defiantly. 'It is my suitcase now. You blundering, stupid ape! I outwitted you once. I can do so again.'

She tried to dodge round the bed and reach the door, but the room was too small and crowded with furniture for anybody however agile to elude a pursuer. Joe caught up with her, threw her across the bed and started beating her with cold ferocity. He beat her with the edge of his hand on her breasts and across her kidneys until she screamed with agony. He jammed his handkerchief into her mouth to reduce the volume by a few decibels and paused for breath.

'Where is it?' he demanded inexorably.

Yvonne rolled her dark eyes with hate-filled defiance and tried to spit at him through the gag. The beating continued with systematic bestiality. He knew all the places on a woman's anatomy where maximum pain could be inflicted with a fairly economical output of energy. Her face was still unmarked after he had beaten her half to death. Yvonne was a quivering, moaning mass of pain, but she would not yield up her secret. She was tough, resilient and stubborn. She had a truly heroic tenacity when it came to hanging on to her money. Bearing pain, especially from men's inhumanity, she accepted fatalistically as her role in life. It was cold, grinding, demoralising poverty that she could not accept. She'd seen her mother ground down into slovenly apathy and despair by a shiftless, bullying Irish drunk. Yvonne would rather die in agony many times over than be as poor as that. Also she had Alain to consider as a prime motive for her resistance. If Blackstock went to the flat in the Rue Tournafort to find the money, and clashed with Alain who would be there packing for his departure, her lover might suffer injury or even worse from that violent criminal.

She fainted under the beating, but still she wouldn't talk. Joe revived her with cold water from the pitcher on the old-fashioned wash-handstand and went to work on her again, but her endurance was phenomenal.

During a rest period he made a

thorough search of her room, but there was no sign of his suitcase. He found the few thousand francs which she kept by her for day-to-day expenses, but there was no trace of the ninety-odd thousand pounds sterling he knew she must have.

He slit open the cheap flock mattress on her bed. He tested every floorboard to see if it had been prised loose recently. He meticulously examined every wardrobe, cupboard and drawer, but all in vain. The little bitch had successfully hidden it somewhere away from her *pension* room, and he was getting nowhere in trying to make her tell where. Was it possible she'd left it with her lover? mused Joe. Or was she, with her own deep self-knowledge of human depravity, too cunning to trust even a lover with such a sum?

When he recollected how close and affectionate she'd behaved towards Alain in that bistro, how she'd looked up at him with the adoring, uncritical eyes of a faithful hound, how they'd walked off arm in arm and parted with a lingering kiss, he thought it was entirely probable that she was sufficiently infatuated even to suspend her mercenary cynicism as far as Alain was concerned. A woman's reproductive system did damned queer things to her judgment and Yvonne was very much a woman who was hooked on *La Différence*. He didn't think there would be any other place in Paris where she would dare hide her hot money but Alain Doumont's flat. So Joe's next course of action must be to go and turn that drum over, before Alain did the obvious thing and took off for Hong Kong with the jackpot.

Yvonne was still unconscious after being systematically beaten insensible, revived and beaten again for over an hour. Joe went hurriedly through her handbag looking for keys. He was gambling on the probability that she might have a key to Alain's flat, as they were on such close and loving terms, and his deduction proved to be correct. He found two big old-fashioned mortise keys in her handbag as well as the two small keys to her suitcase. One mortise key fitted the door to her *pension* room, so the other older and larger key probably fitted the outer door of Alain's flat.

He carefully locked Yvonne in her room, partly because he didn't want her to rush out to a telephone as soon as she regained consciousness and possibly warn Alain; partly because he wanted to keep her safe so that he could come back to work on her again if he drew blank at Alain's flat. He was determined not to let up on Yvonne until he'd recovered his money or killed her in the attempt. Even tough peasants had their breaking-point.

He took a taxi to the Rue Tournefort and stopped outside the tall shuttered house where he'd watched Alain go to ground so many times. In the gloomy entrance passage on the distempered wall was a row of small wooden panels naming the occupant of each flat in the house, telling him as if he didn't know already that M. Doumont lived in Numéro Six.

The old ill-natured concierge came grumbling and croaking out of her witch's den and was about to ask him with characteristic French grace of manner what the hell he wanted, when Joe handed her a fifty-franc note. Her ill-natured truculence died in her heart and she went off muttering.

Joe climbed the three flights of steep stairs. The house was damp and musty and ripe with the medley of strong, strange smells in old French houses: stale coffee, wistful miasmas of long-dead perfume, cooking oil and drains. Everything badly needed a coat of paint. On the third landing he stopped outside Numéro Six and inserted Yvonne's key in the door lock. Miraculously it turned easily and the heavy old door swung back on creaking hinges.

Joe wasn't anticipating any trouble. He knew that at that cosy hour in the afternoon Alain would be locked in a good old clinch with his socially desirable mistress in the Rue Mebillon. Alain's flat was shuttered and dark and looked as if it was lived in by someone untidy and just a bit sleazy. The predominant odours were of stale scent, tobacco, old clothes, honest sweat and a serious lack of fresh air.

Joe walked down the gloomy passage and went by instinct to the lumber-room, the door of which had been left half open by someone in a hurry. As he was about to start searching for his suitcase, he had a strange intuitive feeling that he was not alone. Like most people addicted to the drug of pure excitement, he could sense menace in the air before he even saw it. Something told him he was in appalling danger and that for the first and only time in his colourful life he had run right out of luck.

A harsh, uncouth, guttural voice behind him broke the oppressive silence: 'M'sieu' Alain Doumont?'

René Bruard always followed scrupulously the assassin's honourable punctilio of shooting his victims down eyeball to eyeball. He'd never yet shot anyone in the back, except for a few dozen fellaghas, and they didn't count as human.

Joe wheeled round and saw a stocky figure in a black beret, shabbily dressed, with a sunburnt face the colour of old teak, disfigured by a hideous scar. The revolting apparition also carried a pistol in its right hand. René Bruard had crept past the concierge's room on catlike feet without her hearing or seeing a thing. He'd been waiting in an alcove on the dark landing for Alain Doumont to come home. When a man of roughly the same age as Doumont with much the same build and physical characteristics arrived at the flat and unlocked the door like a bona fide tenant, the assassin did not bother to go into the finer points of his identification. He merely followed him in to finish earning his hundred thousand francs from the cuckold colonel. The weapon in his hand was a very effective tool for the job, a .45 automatic fitted with a potlike silencer.

'*Non!*' cried Joe in desperate panic. '*Pas moi! Ce n'est pas moi!*'

Before he could say another word or even make a move, René Bruard fired three rapid shots, a soft, vicious-sounding phut, phut, phut! barely noticeable outside the room. He was an expert assassin and placed his shots in a neat group, one through the heart, one through the lungs, one through the throat. Joe Blackstock was hurled backwards across the junk-room by the impact of the heavy slugs.

He knew and understood nothing. He died within five seconds, blown away by a low-class French criminal who couldn't even be bothered to verify that he had the right victim.

René didn't trouble to inspect the corpse, not even to rob it. He politely kicked the door of the junk-room shut on his handiwork, walked out of the flat and locked the outer door behind him. Once again he passed as silently as a wraith in his rubber-soled brothel-creepers out through the front hallway without being seen by the concierge. Unhurriedly he walked to where he'd left his baby Honda two streets away and then went chugging off to the Pont Alexandre 3rd to drop the key and the pistol in the middle of the Seine. Then he returned home to await the rest of his blood-money from the colonel before setting out to spend a holiday with an old soldier comrade at the Cours St. Louis near Canebière in Marseilles.

'*Eh, bien, M'sieu' Le Cocu*, your woman is your own again, for a short time!' chuckled René to himself with smug satisfaction.

When Yvonne recovered consciousness she felt so weak and ill she thought she was going to die. Waves of nausea swept over her and she vomited yet again. But after a period of resting the tough resilience of her youth reasserted itself and she realised she wasn't paralysed as she had at first feared. She wasn't going to die either. She had all the world to live for now.

She struggled painfully to her feet and almost sobbed with relief and joy at the realisation that her enemy had gone. She had defeated him by her courage, that foul animal *anglais*. It never occurred to her even when she found her keys missing that Joe knew all about her connection with Alain Doumont and had gone straight to Alain's flat looking for the money.

When she found herself locked in, she put her head through the window overlooking the street and screamed like someone demented until she attracted the attention of a passer-by in the street, who went in and told the keeper of the *pension*, who came upstairs with much grumbling to set her free.

Yvonne was happy for she still had plenty of time to keep her rendezvous with Alain at the Gare de Lyon as they had arranged. She still felt ill from her beating and her body ached all over, but her indomitable spirit rose above all that. At least Blackstock hadn't disfigured her face or damaged her teeth. She could be thankful to him for that.

She was waiting under the booming dome of the Gare de Lyon in good time to meet her lover. Scanning the teeming faces eagerly, she felt the first sick pangs of anxiety as the appointed hour drew near with no sign of Alain.

The train bound for the Cote d'Azur that they should have been aboard roared out of the station and gradually she faced up to the despairing thought that she would never see Alain again. She understood it all now. She had been a naive trusting imbecile to tell him her great secret. He was just a filthy crook like all the rest. He had gone for good and so had all her beautiful money.

She sat down on the new suitcase that contained her honeymoon trousseau and wept unrestrainedly in full view of the unconcerned, unfeeling passers-by, rushing for their trains.

Eventually she pulled herself together and went by taxi to the Rue Tournefort in a last desperate hope that perhaps Alain had been unavoidably delayed and she had misjudged him. But his flat was locked up and Blackstock had taken her key away when he rifled her handbag. There was no answer to her frenzied cries and pounding on the door. The silence of death hung over it.

As Yvonne came downstairs the concierge came wheezing up to her, rubbing her arthritic hands.

'*Vous cherchez quelque chose, Mademoiselle*,' she croaked maliciously, understanding well enough that Yvonne had been stood up.

The old woman then gleefully informed her that she hadn't seen M. Doumont since the early afternoon when he had rushed out in a very great hurry.

'Was he carrying a white suitcase?'

'He had two suitcases, Mademoiselle. One of them was white.'

Yvonne walked broken and disconsolate away. She had taken that awful beating from Blackstock all for nothing. After all that planning, achievement and suffering she was poor again. A chance of immense riches like the Blackstock bank haul would never come again in her lifetime. There was no suitable job for her in France. She would have to go back to that dreary England and work as a secretary or stewardess for another airline, she who had once been as wealthy as a queen.

As for men in her life, she would punish every man she knew henceforth and screw everything she could out of him. She would beat them all at their own dirty game. Alain Doumont was just a filthy piece of *merde*, and if she ever set eyes on him again she would risk everything to dose him with rat poison or slip a poniard between his ribs.

19

After the awful débâcle of trying to steal Joe Blackstock's suitcase in the Montana Hotel at Basle, Rowland Seaton was injured far more deeply than by the superficial manifestations of a cut lip, two black eyes and a badly swollen jaw. His macho image in his own eyes and in the eyes of his woman had taken a fearful tumble. No longer could he appear in Sally's eyes as the dashing, debonair hero figure, who always won his chivalrously fought bouts with a sordid world. In their fracas Blackstock had shown him up as an incompetent thief and an inferior contender on a squalid battle-ground of Seaton's own choosing.

Although Sally did not love him the less for his humiliating defeat in an ignominious enterprise, she now had to face the fact that her beloved idol had feet of clay. Rollo was enraged even more venomously when he saw her looking at him in a tenderly pitying and maternal way instead of with the reverential adoration he demanded as his due. He snarled and cursed her when she tried to console him and advised soothing remedies for his bruised face, like a loving mother with a battered toddler.

Rollo was a splendid hater. Nothing would satisfy him now but a final shattering revenge on Joe Blackstock, whatever the cost to himself in blood and strife. He felt in some strange twisted way that destroying Joe Blackstock would restore his own heroic image in his own and Sally's eyes. Rollo Seaton and Joe Blackstock were too much alike and had known each other too long and too well for the hatred not to be mortal. War between two strangers over money would have been relatively clean and chivalrous.

'I'm going to fix that crooked bastard so that his luck runs out for good,' vowed Rollo murderously.

'Oh darling,' pleaded Sally fearfully, 'why can't you forget Blackstock? A brutal thug like him is bound to bring about his own downfall sooner or later. So why risk compromising the whole of our happiness together just to hasten the process by a year of two? What does Blackstock matter, one way or the other?'

'You don't understand,' snapped Rollo. 'How could you? You're just a woman. It's a vital principle of male self-respect at stake here. Nobody trips me up and kicks me in the face while I'm down without getting the return match with knobs on.'

'If you say so, darling,' she sighed.

Sally had a worrying feminine premonition that another brutal clash with Joe Blackstock could lead only to a worse disaster and more serious injury for Rollo. He just wasn't in the same league for slick villainy and destructive violence as the professional robber and con man. Sally couldn't bear to think of Rollo's ever meeting him again.

'The way I see it,' said Rollo complacently, 'all we've got to do is give doddering old blind Justice a little nudge in the right direction to deliver that lousy bastard his come-uppance for the Dulwich robbery.'

'Oh Rollo, you don't mean inform the police?'

'Better than that,' replied Rollo smugly. 'I can give them actual material proof that Blackstock knocked over that security van and ripped off two hundred grand.'

'How?'

'Like I told you, in payment for his air fare he gave me some bundles of brand new unwrapped notes, tenners, and I've not spent it all yet. Well, their serial numbers will all be on record as stolen, so anybody caught with a few bundles is really for the high jump.'

Sally was dismayed and frightened.

'Oh, please don't do anything so foolish, Rollo. If you should be caught in possession of that money, you'll be taken for as big a villain as Blackstock is.'

'All we've got to do is plant a few hundred of the stolen bread in Blackstock's pad, and then give an anonymous tip-off to the fuzz about where to look.'

'We!' she said aghast. 'Rollo, it may be

223

worthy of Blackstock, but certainly not of you. And I want no part in it.'

'The only snag is I don't know Blackstock's home address,' mused Rollo. 'It's somewhere in Belgravia, and his telephone number is ex-directory. Not to worry though. I see another way to get to him. I know he works hand-in-glove with Vic Mannion at pulling all these money-making strokes, and I know Mannion's palace in Hampstead. One of these days we'll go and deliver a little parcel to old Vic, and say we were asked to smuggle it back on the plane to Joe, but we don't know where he lives, so would good old Vic hang on to it and hand it over? Then when we tip them off and the cavalry come romping up to turn over Vic's pad, and Vic realises he's been framed, he's not going to be very pleased with his partner for causing it to happen. Perhaps out of that little distrust and resentment, the two villains will eventually turn on each other and honest men will come into their own.'

He went on elaborating his plan with growing enthusiasm, working it out in detail and explaining to Sally how she was going to help him put it into practice. Although she argued and resisted, she gave way to him in the end as she always did. When once Rollo started to make love to her, all her moral and discretionary considerations were abruptly neutralised. His expert caresses destroyed her will power and made her fatalistic. She would do anything in the world to please him, even participate in his malicious sortie of revenge which her deep intuition told her they would both bitterly regret.

* * *

Some weeks later the pilot and his stewardess wangled a few days' leave together and instead of going to their respective homes they arranged to spend it together at a hotel near Victoria Station called the New Caledonian. It was small, dowdy, back-street-respectable, and reasonably priced compared with the more fashionable tourist traps. They took a room there under the name of Mr and

Mrs Jeffs, which by Sally's reckoning did not sound as naughty as Smith.

On a mild October evening Sally Crowther arrived by taxi at Victor Mannion's house in Hampstead to make a preliminary reconnaissance, to test the old villain's susceptibility to her charms and if possible capture his trust as well as his desire.

As it happened Vic was emotionally wide open to such a foray, for he'd recently lost the home comforts of Erika Fontaine. Without a qualm or a backwards glance she'd transferred her favours to a suave Italian club manager in Mayfair, who had the reputation of sinister connections with a New York Family and could offer a girl far more in cash and in kind even than Vic Mannion could provide. Adding insult to injury she'd walked off with the valuable mink coat Vic had given her, as well as all the items of costly jewellery that his lustful uxoriousness had showered on her, to the value of about ten thousand pounds.

This domestic disaster had come at a time when Vic was still fretting over his costly failure to eliminate the Supergrass who threatened his partnership, and was also becoming increasingly worried about the fate of all the money which Joe Blackstock had taken to bank in Switzerland.

It was now five weeks since Joe had taken off and, apart from an initial phone call from Basle to inform Vic that he'd arrived safely and everything was going according to plan, nothing more had been heard from him. This prolonged silence from his partner was so unlike Joe's usual procedure that Vic felt in his bones something had gone badly wrong. Either Joe had come to grief tangling with the police or other predators who'd smelt out the large amount of cash he had with him, or else Joe had double-crossed his partner. Maybe he'd decided to settle permanently abroad in view of the danger he was now in from Tom Garbutt's turning Supergrass. In which case he would need the full two hundred grand to set him up after leaving behind all his assets in England. As he would never see Vic Mannion again, why should he even consider the wrath of his former partner? Vic felt his blood pressure rising with insane rage even at the thought of it. The only tangible asset he had from the Dulwich bank raid which he'd master-minded was Joe Blackstock's XJS Jaguar, now worth about fifteen thousand pounds.

When Vic's doorbell rang and he came face to face with Sally Crowther, Vic was so enthralled that he momentarily forgot all the bad things that had happened or were about to happen. Sally was an alluring vision with her expensively coiffeured blonde hair, her shimmering, sheath-like party dress, with a mink stole round her bare shoulders. She introduced herself with a dignified *savoir faire* and a slight aloofness.

'Mr Mannion? I hope you won't think it terribly presumptuous of me for calling on you like this. I'm a friend of Joe Blackstock's. We met in Switzerland last week, and he told me you'd be pleased to see me when I next came to London.'

'Really?' exclaimed Vic with an enormous feeling of delight and relief at the news from this enchanting emissary that his fears about Joe had been unfounded.

'Well, that's marvellous. I'm always pleased to see any friend of Joe. How is the old devil, then?'

'You mean you haven't seen him recently?' said Sally in some surprise.

'Not since he left for Switzerland over a month ago. You say you saw him there last week?'

'Yes, I was staying at the Montana Hotel in Basle while he was there, and we became rather friendly. He spoke with great warmth about you, said you were a kind of father figure to him and practically made me promise to look you up in Hampstead.'

'No message?' said Vic eagerly.

'No. Just me in person.'

The guarded expression of teasing and challenge in her eyes told him that with this visit she had something more positive in mind than a mere platonic 'Hello'. Joe had sent him a real bonus with this one as if he understood his partner's deepest need. This could be Vic's true and definitive Indian summer.

'Well,' he said grandly, 'you're obviously dressed for a party, so let me take you to one. You're not booked up, are you?'

'No,' she said hesitantly. 'What had you in mind?'

'What about somewhere quiet for a meal, and then maybe a club afterwards?'

'What a lovely idea! A girl loves sudden surprises. It's obvious you're a man of instant bold decisions.'

'You stick with me then' blustered Vic, his voice heavy with desire. 'You've seen nothing yet.'

Sally was too experienced not to read his intent. She understood him intuitively as an aggressive, amorous brute of a man, a spoilt child who'd never been effectively slapped down, a veteran stallion who saw it as his unchallenged prerogative to enjoy every comely filly who came his way. She was a bit afraid of what she was getting involved in as she saw the undistinguished lust in his closeset green eyes and felt his hot heavy paw on her bare arm. But she was also strangely exhilarated, for she'd never been desired before by a man of Vic Mannion's animal magnetism and menacing power.

She sat as far away from him as possible in the taxi going down to the West End and tried to frown on his possessive way of pawing her about, but she found herself secretly enjoying it when his hot hand fell heavily on her knee. When he took her into Trader Vic's under the Hilton, he behaved as if he owned it, and was on first-name terms with the charismatic waiters, who bowed them obsequiously to a secluded table with shaded lights. Sally was amused at the childish pleasure of her bull-like escort in his eagerness to show he was a favoured tycoon who had everybody in his pocket.

Before long he was telling her the edited story of his life, romanticising his humble origins and injecting a note of pathos into the sufferings of his early years: how his trusting and unworldly father was cheated of his birthright by a shower of scheming kikes. He described his own early preoccupation with the struggle for power; how he'd survived the lean years of austerity after the war, working on a fairground and saving every penny to start his own business. He carefully omitted the unsavoury episode of a six-month prison sentence for stealing lead from the roof of a bomb-damaged church in East London.

'So what about you then, darling?' said the old ram, running his index-finger playfully round her nipple. 'I've told you the story of my life. Don't I get to know yours? You might have landed in Hampstead from outer space for all I know about you. Where do you live, for instance? Are you married, separated, divorced? What exactly were you doing in Switzerland when you met Joe, and how much of a friend were you to him?'

'Questions, questions,' she said with a provocative smile. 'If you knew all that had ever happened to me, you couldn't be blamed for trying to make it happen again.'

He glanced at her slyly and chuckled, wondering how far she'd proved satisfactory to Joe and exactly why Joe had passed her over to him.

'You're telling me you've got plenty to hide,' he observed.

'Hasn't everybody past the age of fifteen?'

'Why don't you let me take you to a club and try your hand at the Casino? You might have a winning streak and show me where to place my chips.'

'Oh no. I don't have that sort of money.'

'I'll stake you.'

'Thank you, but I couldn't possibly. I've no interest in gambling, but I'll go along with you and watch, if you're determined to waste your money on the tables.'

'Good girl,' said Vic, squeezing her thigh under the table.

* * *

Back at the house in Hampstead Vic presented her with a heavy gold bangle that Erika had somehow managed to leave behind in her hasty absconding with the loot.

'With strings or without?' said Sally.

'No strings. I don't buy my women. If they don't like me for what I am, they can do the other thing. Why should I waste my last remaining strength in forcing a reluctant woman, when there are so many deprived women about who really need a favour?'

'I don't know what the new generation of women's libbers would make of that piece of male chauvinism,' remarked Sally, caressing the mellow gold bangle lovingly. 'But I forgive you for being such a nice man. You can be nice to me if you like.'

After Vic had made love to her in his powerful, ruthless and effective way, she mentally marked down Rollo Seaton's somewhat kinky and effete performance a few points by the new standard she'd discovered. She was so relaxed and yielding with warm affection for Vic Mannion that she was on the point of giving him her whole confidence, blurting out the truth of Rollo's seedy revenge plot to get to Joe Blackstock through his partner in crime and destroy him. She had to concentrate very hard on

Rollo's glamour, his pilot's wings and the scrambled egg on his cap in order to stay loyal to him.

In the end old habit and prudence reasserted themselves. She kept quiet because she was afraid of Vic's reaction. He might turn on her savagely and beat her up for her initial treachery. Or he might use his criminal contacts to turn the tables on poor Rollo and bring about his destruction. In the revealing moments of coition she had glimpsed Vic's elemental savagery. She could never forget for long the original Dulwich robbery which, by such devious means, had brought her here and thrown her into Mannion's arms. He was a dangerous criminal to whom in the last analysis human values counted for nothing. To throw in her lot with him could only result in terrible grief and pain. There was nothing more to this old Mannion than a glorious ride. He'd bought her favours with a gold bangle, but he hadn't talked about any deeper relationship or offered her anything permanent.

Now that she could think straight again

she knew that for better or worse she was tied to the weaker, less masculine, less effectual Rollo Seaton. She avoided Vic's eyes with a feeling of cheapness and shame as she left his bed, gathered up her clothes and walked naked into the adjoining bathroom to shower away all traces of his physical contact.

Vic stared after her with wistful regret. It had been very much in Vic's mind as his wild love mounted to its climax to make a permanency of this relationship, to invite Sally into his home to fill the aching physical need that Erika had left. Sally had more class as well as more kindness than that dirty little slag who'd robbed him blind, and she couldn't fail to adorn his home, the envy of all his associates.

But when his pulse-beat had subsided and cold rationality returned, he realised she was still as closed-in and secretive as when she'd first walked out of the night into his house. Was she just a whimsical courtesan who lived for the pleasure of the moment, grabbed what was going and then moved on to the next adventure? Or

236

was she after something else? Could she be up to something dodgy that would only become apparent when she'd taken him to the cleaners in some deep and cunning way? Then there was the Joe Blackstock factor in the equation. If Joe had been in Switzerland up to a week ago, why had he kept incommunicado for so long? Was he really planning to double-cross Vic over the money? Why had he really sent this superior broad to tie one on for Vic at his Hampstead home? There was something going down that Vic couldn't fathom, and anything that wasn't clear in the open had a smell to it.

However, Sally was a lot of fun in the sack and that in itself never did a man any harm. Vic might as well grab all she was offering and drag out his Indian summer as lingeringly as possible for as long as Sally stayed on the loose and fancy-free in London.

When she'd showered and dressed he phoned for a taxi to take her home. As she took her leave he offered to meet her at Trader Vic's for lunch next day and after demurring for a bit she allowed herself to be persuaded. It was three a.m. when she arrived back at the New Caledonian Hotel in Victoria and paid off the taxi. She guiltily concealed Vic's gift of the gold bangle in the bottom of her handbag before she went upstairs. Rollo was certainly not rational or fair-minded enough to be tolerant of the friendly little contract by which she'd obtained it, even though he'd given her direct orders to make Mannion eat out of her hand.

She found Rollo in their hotel room lying restlessly on top of the bed chain-smoking, with an ash-tray full of ash and burnt-out stubs beside him and an empty Scotch-bottle rolling about at the foot of the bed.

'Where the hell have you been?' he demanded accusingly. 'I told you just to chat him up and win his confidence, not make a bloody night of it.'

'I just did as you told me,' she replied curtly. 'If I'm to hobnob with the Devil I need a long spoon. You can't regulate such an operation by remote control.'

'Don't be bloody clever. What have you been doing for the last seven hours?'

'Playing roulette.'

'What! Where?'

'A club in Mayfair called the Locarno.'

'Oh yes? What did you use for money?'

'Mr Mannion said he'd stake me because I'd probably bring him luck.'

'A likely story! And did you bring him luck?'

'Beginners' luck. At one point I was several hundred pounds ahead. Then the bug got to me and I went on doubling up till I lost the lot.'

'You bloody fool!' swore Rollo in disgust. 'Why didn't you cash in and come away while you were still winning?'

'You told me to win his confidence. If I'd acted like a greedy harpy, walking off with my winnings like a professional casino crawler, he wouldn't trust me. As it is he's asked me to have lunch with him again tomorrow at the Hilton.'

'Well, that can't be bad,' conceded Rollo. 'He must be keen. Did you go to bed with him?'

'No,' said Sally, meeting his eyes with

a clear innocent gaze. 'He wanted me to and pressured me very hard, but I managed to stall him with a half-promise. Maybe tomorrow, maybe.'

'Bloody good show,' approved Rollo. 'I wouldn't have sent you to him if I hadn't known you were extra good at keeping your legs crossed. It sounds as if you've got him nicely hooked. Did you mention the brief-case that Joe Blackstock asked you to bring through the customs for him?'

'No. I thought I'd better ask you about that because apparently Blackstock hasn't come back yet. Mannion said he hasn't heard from him for over a month.'

'The hell he hasn't!' muttered Rollo with quickening interest. 'I wonder what the bent bastard's up to out there. Not to worry. It makes our job easier. It'll sound more convincing that Blackstock who's not coming back yet asked you to deliver the brief-case to his partner to look after for him till he does get back.'

'All right,' said Sally reluctantly. 'But I still think it's a low-down dirty trick.'

'It's a low-down dirty world, and not of my making,' replied Rollo complacently. 'And we're in the virtuous business of teaching those fat crooks that crime doesn't pay.'

'I wish I had your easy conscience. Old Mannion seems a decent enough man in his uncouth way. He can't help it if he never went to posh schools like you and Blackstock.'

'Don't you go falling for that bloody old criminal,' exploded Rollo vehemently. 'I suppose he gave you his vulgar blarney and splashed his pirate's gold about, and you fell for it like all the women do.'

'It wasn't like that at all.'

'He's a bloody bank robber, a fixer of organised crime, and don't you ever forget it. I'd like to know where he's hiding his share of the Dulwich heist till he can get it laundered. Perhaps you can lure him away from his pad one night while I get in there and give it a going-over.'

'Not on your life!' replied Sally firmly. 'Remember what happened in Basle? Next time you might really come

241

unstuck, and it'll take more than a few cold compresses to repair the damage.'

'Oh balls!' exclaimed Rollo angrily. 'You never let anything drop, do you? Hurry up and come to bed. I'm feeling extra fruity tonight, so fasten your seat-belt and give me take-off power!'

20

Detective Chief Superintendent Pritchard of the Robbery Squad had now spent several interesting sessions listening to the colourful memoirs and breezy confessions of Supergrass Tom Garbutt, who'd named names and specified times and places. The chief superintendent now badly wanted to interview Joseph James Blackstock of Belgravia, to help him with his enquiries into several spectacular armed robberies in and around the capital during the past two years. An urgent directive had gone out to bring him in for questioning, but Joe Blackstock was nowhere to be found in his usual haunts. He was thought vaguely to be in Europe on business, so Interpol had been alerted to hold him for questioning. So far however, no sighting of him was reported anywhere. Nor was there a trace of the two hundred thousand pounds that Garbutt swore he'd stolen on the Dulwich security van raid.

Frustrated in this direction, the chief superintendent started looking hopefully towards Victor Mannion, who was still very much alive and thriving in Hampstead. The trouble was that Garbutt had no positive knowledge of Mannion's involvement in the robberies. All he'd heard was a muttered rumour, a hearsay whisper that Mannion was Blackstock's partner who did most of the intelligence work and the organising of their spectacular robberies.

Hearsay alone was not sufficient justification to swear out a warrant and go searching Mannion's house. The detective could fall flat on his face and incur justifiable complaints from Mannion's high-powered lawyer if he acted with no supportive evidence. The law would be on Mannion's side and he was too tough to crack under police interrogation. So the chief superintendent decided to put a long-range surveillance on Mannion and wait patiently for Blackstock or some of the other villains to contact him when they thought the heat was cooling.

The watch on Mannion, called discretionary surveillance, was so low-key and unobtrusive that Vic had no idea of the familiar spirit who always had him in sight when he spent a day at the races or a night in a Mayfair club, or squired an elderly film star to a charity flower show, like a well loved pillar of the community. It was Detective Chief Superintendent Pritchard's declared policy to let him crawl unharmed into the woodwork and feel safe, so that when his itching greed and love of a good deal prompted him to set up another well organised raid on Society's wealth, the Robbery Squad would be well in the picture.

At midday when Vic arrived to meet his new love outside the Park Lane Hilton, he was under the jaundiced and hostile scrutiny of a Scotland Yard detective two hundred yards away, equipped with powerful binoculars and a two-way radio tuned in directly to a receiver in DCS Pritchard's office at the Yard.

When Sally appeared in the foyer she

was carrying a small leather brief-case which was locked and for which she did not possess a key. After exchanging cordial greetings with Vic and accepting his offer of a pre-lunch Martini, she said:

'I'm wondering what I ought to do with this brief-case belonging to Joe Blackstock. He asked me to bring it into England for him and deliver it to him at his flat in Belgravia. Well, I've been to his place a couple of times and it's all locked up. There's nobody there. I feel responsible for seeing that it gets safely into Joe's hands, so what do you think I ought to do with it? Should I leave it at home till Joe contacts me, or should I leave it at the left-luggage office at a railway station?'

Vic frowned with vague uneasiness as he stared first at Sally and then at the innocuous-looking little leather case she was carrying. He knew the kind of merchandise that Joe generally imported into the country, using a stooge as courier.

Sally met his gaze, frank, innocent and

246

unperturbed. She obviously didn't regard the brief-case as a source of danger and she was a very lovely girl.

'Have you got any idea what's in it?' he asked.

'No, I haven't a clue. It's locked and Joe's got the key.'

'Didn't the customs blokes want to open it up?'

'No. They were on a go-slow and waved everybody through with a lordly air. If I'd been openly carrying a case of brandy they wouldn't have charged me any duty on it.'

'Well, I don't know what to suggest you do with it.'

'You see,' said Sally, 'I'm so afraid of losing it. You've no idea how forgetful I am, leaving parcels behind in shops after I've paid for them, going shopping without money or my Access Card. I'd never forgive myself if I lost Joe's brief-case after he trusted it to me. Besides. I'll be going to my job in Brussels in a few days, and that means leaving it at my parents' house. Oh dear! More complications.'

Vic looked at her again uncertainly, realising he knew absolutely nothing about her except that she was a marvellous lay. But Joe seemed to trust her and, if he'd asked her to bring that brief-case into England, it must be worth looking after. It might not be a bad idea to hold something valuable of Joe's, just in case he was keeping all the money he'd exported.

'Perhaps you'd better leave the brief-case with me,' he offered grudgingly. 'I've got a safe-deposit a box at the bank where I can keep it till Joe shows his face again. It'll be a hundred per cent safe there.'

'Oh, would you really?' said Sally with deep gratitude. 'You've no idea what a load off my mind that will be.'

She handed the brief-case to him with obvious relief and they went in to lunch: Scotch salmon, fillet steak, strawberries and cream accompanied by two bottles of champagne. Enjoying his food with his usual gusto, Vic kept glancing at the brief-case he'd acquired. He was burning with curiosity to know what was in it, but he couldn't very well break it open there in the Trader Vic Restaurant with a knife and fork. He would have to take it home before he buried it in his safe-deposit box.

After lunch Vic paid the bill, picked up his hat and gloves and the brief-case. Sally took a cordial leave of him and went off to do some personal shopping in Oxford Street. She'd promised to come to the house in Hampstead again that evening to be wined and dined and lovingly assaulted and fulfilled in the old Pasha's seraglio. At least that was Vic's understanding of her implied promise. But Sally had already secretly decided that she'd never see him again. The transfer of that treacherous package must mean that henceforth they would be mortal enemies. She felt dreadful in the role of traitor and decoy, coming to a man in the guise of friendship to destroy him, like Judas Iscariot with his famous kiss. She would be glad to get back to her regular job with the airline and forget all this squalid play-acting after Rollo had got over his crazy obsession for revenge and was himself again.

The Robbery Squad detective in his nondescript little, car, parked in the forecourt of a block of luxury flats, trained his binoculars on the hulking bear-like man in his flashy tweeds, who looked like a bookmaker on the race course, and then on the svelte, well groomed, good-looking blonde in her immaculate two-piece suit as they parted and went their separate ways.

The detective spoke into his transmitter:

'Our man is just leaving the Hilton. The woman has gone off alone. The brief-case seems to have changed hands. She was carrying it when she arrived. Now he's got it.'

'Good!' replied the chief superintendent. 'Pick him up and bring him in. That brief-case could be crucial. We'll have the woman picked up as well.'

As Vic was about to get into his taxi the shabby little car screamed to a halt beside him. A man who was obviously a hard-faced copper, one of the eternal enemy, confronted Vic.

'May I ask you what you have in that

brief-case, sir?' he asked civilly.

'What the hell business is it of yours?' commented Vic, bristling with instant alarm and anger. 'Who are you anyway?'

The detective showed his warrant card and introduced himself.

As soon as he mentioned the ominous words 'Robbery Squad', Vic felt an icy pang of dread and the knowledge that he was sunk.

'How should I know what's in the case?' he blustered. 'It isn't mine anyway. Some broad I hardly know asked me to look after it for her.'

'That being so,' said the detective suavely, 'I must ask you to accompany me to Scotland Yard to help us with out enquiries.'

Vic felt like a trapped animal as he realised that the brief-case must contain a deadly load. So that was it! A perfect frame-up, and he'd fallen for it! He should have known Sally was too good to be true. She was a treacherous enemy who'd come in the guise of love to sell him down the river. His Indian summer of romance was to close with a stinging and killing frost. Somehow it seemed infinitely worse that she'd got to him by using Joe Blackstock's credentials. Then with a shock of dread and a terrible insight it dawned on him that perhaps it was Joe who'd set the whole thing up to have him put away. If Joe had planned to rob his partner of the Dulwich bonanza, it made good tactical sense to destroy his victim by a neat deadly frame-up so that there could be no retaliation.

Vic was so furious and desperate that he was tempted to slug the young copper and make a run for it, to stay at liberty long enough to find Joe Blackstock and exact a terrible revenge. But Vic's sprinting days were over and, in the middle of Park Lane in broad daylight with radios blaring and squad cars homing in, what chance would he have?

The detective took possession of the suspect brief-case and Vic allowed himself to be driven off to Scotland Yard. They showed him into DCS Pritchard's office where the all too familiar scene was set.

'Hullo, Mr Mannion,' said Pritchard genially, getting to his feet behind the desk. 'I've not had the pleasure of meeting you before, but I have a feeling we're going to have a great deal in common. Before you say a word it's my duty to give you the official caution, as I'm sure you are aware.'

He intoned the hateful words which Vic hadn't heard for a good many years but which reminded him of where he'd always stood, on the wrong side of the fence.

'Of course you'll want your solicitor present for the few routine questions we have to put to you,' continued the chief superintendent sympathetically. 'So until he gets here why don't we get a locksmith to open up your brief-case and see what's in it?'

'It's not my brief-case, I keep telling you,' fumed Vic, hoarse with rage. 'I disclaim ownership of it. It was planted on me by that lousy woman, a frame-up pure and simple. I don't know who the hell she is or why she's out to get me, but by God she's got some explaining to do.'

'Oddly enough that's what we feel

about her too,' agreed Pritchard. 'We've been most interested in her ever since she appeared at your house in Hampstead yesterday evening to make contact with you. She's staying at the New Caledonian Hotel only a couple of streets from here with some bloke who calls himself Jeffs. Don't worry, Mr Mannion. We'll soon know who she is and what she's got against you.'

The police locksmith in his clean white coat with his bag of delicate surgical instruments set to work on the briefcase and released the lock in a couple of minutes without even scratching it. He tipped out on the chief superintendent's desk a thin sheaf of crisp new ten-pound notes, a hundred pounds in all, which Rollo had been able to spare from his own part of the haul.

Pritchard glanced at the serial numbers in sequence and checked them against one of the lists of the still missing bank notes whose numbers had been provided by the issuing bank after the robbery.

'Very interesting,' he observed dryly with the calm satisfaction of a policeman who sees his victim in the net. 'This money is part of the two hundred thousand pounds that was stolen last month in Dulwich when a security van was stopped and robbed and two of the guards were blinded with ammonia. We've had you in mind as a possible suspect, and my next question is, can you help us to recover the rest of the missing money?'

Vic was almost speechless with shock at the implications of the disaster. The only thing he knew for sure was that the incriminating money could only have been supplied to the woman by Joe Blackstock. It was treachery more diabolical than anything he'd foreseen. However, with automatic recourse to the blocking and defensive tactics he'd always used years ago against the police he muttered:

'I don't know what kind of a bloody frame-up you've organised against me, but you know you won't get away with it. I'm not saying anything else till my brief gets here.'

'That's your privilege of course,' retorted Pritchard. 'We're in no hurry.'

An hour later Reuben Levine arrived at Scotland Yard and was immediately admitted to the Interview Room where Vic was being held. When Vic told him about the mysterious girl from the shadows and her brief-case containing money from the Dulwich robbery, the lawyer pulled a long face.

'I don't like the sound of it at all,' he said. 'I suppose there could be some possibility that this woman is a police decoy, used by them to plant evidence on you so that they could make an arrest. If so, we'll have a few police resignations before we're finished.'

Vic nodded, pretending to take comfort from Levine's bombastic tone, but in his heart he knew Sally was no police decoy.

'Is there anything about this case you haven't told me?' demanded the lawyer sharply. 'If I'm to make a good job of your defence, I don't want Counsel to be made a fool of in court by being confronted with some damning evidence that he never even knew about.'

'Of course there's no damning evidence, apart from that money in the brief-case that the bitch planted on me,' declared Vic passionately. 'Would a man in my position risk everything by getting mixed up in some half-arsed robbery, and then leave evidence lying about all over the place for the fuzz to get hold of?'

'I hope not, Victor,' said Levine, looking at him doubtfully. 'I sincerely hope not.'

When DCS Pritchard came back to confront the suspect and his lawyer, Reuben Levine was on his feet, bright and perky as a cock sparrow, just as if he were already taking the floor in a court of law and had a complete answer to everything.

'My client declines to make a statement, and reserves his defence,' he annouced primly. 'The money found in his possession was planted on him by a woman as yet unknown, for reasons still to be ascertained. It was a clumsy and malicious attempt to incriminate an innocent man. It's inconceivable that you should bring charges against him on those grounds. If you persist, the case won't even get past the Magistrates' Court. So let's put an end to the whole stupid business. I want my client discharged immediately.'

'Not so fast, Mr Levine,' said the chief superintendent unperturbed. 'In view of the stolen money found in your client's possession and the strong presumption of his involvement in the robbery, we shall have to satisfy ourselves that no more of the missing money is in his possession. We shall have to search his house, and in anticipation of it I've already had a search-warrant prepared. I must ask you to come with us to your house, Mr Mannion, while we execute the warrant. I'd like you to come too, Mr Levine, to satisfy yourself that the search is properly conducted.'

'Really, Superintendent, is all this really necessary?' exclaimed Levine, bridling with indignation.

'It's OK,' growled Vic. 'Let 'em search all they want. They won't find anything at my place, not even a bloody reefer. I don't rob banks, and even if I did I wouldn't leave the money under my bed like some incompetent little tea-leaf.'

'Well, that's fine, Mr Mannion,' replied Pritchard courteously. 'Then you have nothing to fear.'

They put Vic in the back of a large Volvo alongside the chief superintendent and drove him out to Hampstead, while Reuben Levine followed the police convoy in his own Rolls-Royce.

A team of experienced detectives searched the house from top to bottom, supervised punctiliously by Levine, while Vic sat confidently in his study and fortified himself with Scotch on the rocks. The chief superintendent declined a drink, but sat and watched him closely.

After they'd searched the house and found nothing incriminating, the detectives moved to the summer house, the other outbuildings and inevitably to the garage. Presently a young detective constable came in and whispered something to the chief superintendent, who sat up with sudden interest.

'That car at the back of your garage, Mr Mannion, the red Jaguar XJS, registration number JB 2, is it yours?'

'No,' replied Vic uneasily.

'Whose is it then?'

'It belongs to a friend of mine. He's out of town at the moment, and as he doesn't have a lock-up garage he was afraid of it getting nicked or vandalised in the city. He asked me to store it here for him.'

'I see. May I ask the name of your friend?'

'What does that matter?' blustered Vic. 'It's just a domestic arrangement. There's no law against storing somebody's car, is there?'

'Indeed not. There's also no harm in revealing the name of that somebody, if he's a peaceful, law-abiding citizen. Just give me the name, Mr Mannion, and save me the trouble of going to the police computer at Hendon to find out who's the registered owner of JB 2.'

'All right,' muttered Vic dejectedly. 'It

belongs to Joe Blackstock. He lives in Belgravia.'

Pritchard's face didn't betray a flicker of emotion.

'How close is your relationship with Mr Blackstock? What kind of business do you carry on together, Mr Mannion?'

'Nothing at all,' replied Vic desperately. 'I just meet him occasionally in a club or on the race-course.'

Pritchard turned to the young detective who was standing by.

'I want that car thoroughly searched. Strip it down to the chassis if you have to. I don't have to tell you what you're looking for.'

The red Jaguar was started up and backed out into the sunlight. While Vic, his lawyer and the chief superintendent looked on, detectives swarmed all over the car. It didn't take a minute for one of them to open the panel to the spare-wheel compartment and reveal all the bundles of newly printed one-pound notes which Joe had been unable to cram into his suitcase.

A silence of shocked incredulity

descended on the assembled company, but on the police side the jubilation was obvious.

'Well, Mr Mannion?' said the chief superintendent briskly. 'And how do you account for all this money on your premises? No, don't say anything yet. In the presence of your solicitor I have to re-administer the official caution. You're not obliged to say anything . . .'

As soon as he saw the bundles of new one-pound notes, the delayed-action bomb that Joe Blackstock had set under him before he took off for Basle, Vic realised that the game was over and he had to put his hands up.

'Of course,' went on the chief superintendent, 'the serial numbers of these notes have yet to be verified against the numbers of those stolen in the Dulwich robbery. If the numbers do tally, you realise the implications for you?'

'Don't say anything!' hissed Reuben Levine, standing at Mannion's elbow. 'My client has no comment to make at this stage, Superintendent. He has a complete answer to all your queries, and his defence will be properly presented at the proper time.'

But Vic already knew he was beaten by Joe's black-hearted treachery. All he could do now was shift some of the blame to where it rightly belonged.

'All right,' he croaked in a stifled voice that didn't sound like his own. 'I'll tell you all I know. I heard a rumour that Blackstock was into armed robbery, but I didn't really believe it. When he rang me up and asked me to store his car for him till he got back from Europe, I had no idea he'd left stolen money hidden in it.'

'I'm quite sure you hadn't,' agreed the chief superintendent cordially. 'But I'm also sure you can tell us a great deal more about your working relationship over the years with Joseph Blackstock.'

Vic realised that all his wriggling and squirming on the hook could only supply occupational therapy for this smug copper who had everything going his way. There was no question of Vic making a deal as a Supergrass, for the police had Joe

Blackstock stitched up already on Tom Garbutt's testimony. All Vic had left to hope for was that when they sent him down he would at least be in the same prison as Blackstock so that he had a goal in life to aim for.

21

Some weeks later, after Vic Mannion had been formally charged with conspiracy to rob a bank security van in Dulwich on September 3rd, and remanded in custody pending the apprehension of his criminal associate and their trial at the Central Criminal Court, Joe Blackstock surfaced in Paris.

The concierge at the flats in the Rue Tournefort rang her local Gendarmerie and insisted that something was badly wrong in Numéro Six. The regular occupant hadn't been seen for many weeks and in the mild weather a strange and horrible smell had become evident on the landing outside Numéro Six. It grew stronger every day and the tenants on the floors above and below were all complaining about the stench as a health hazard. The old woman said she was afraid to go in there herself for fear of what she might find.

The police came and used her master key to open the outer door of Numéro Six. They found the badly decomposing body of a man and the forensic experts who worked on the scene had to wear breathing apparatus. The cause of death by gunshot wounds was quickly established. The dead man carried no passport or other means of identification, but the detectives from the *Sûreté Nationale* immediately deduced from the label of the famous Savile Row tailor inside his suit that the victim was probably an Englishman. He was certainly not Alain Doumont, the regular Parisian occupant of the flat, for Doumont's elderly father, summoned to identify the body, stoutly maintained it was not his son. The police badly wanted to interview Alain Doumont, who was nowhere to be found, so they put out a nationwide and European alert to have him detained.

Since the dead man's finger-ends were not as yet too badly decomposed to yield specimen prints to the finger-print experts, copies of the prints were sent to Scotland Yard, who quickly ascertained that the dead man in the Rue Tournefort was Joseph James Blackstock, a client of the Criminal Records Office, who was wanted for questioning in London. The Robbery Squad men were very peeved that they'd just got back a hunk of rotting carrion in Paris, with no vestige of the stolen loot.

Shortly afterwards, however, Alain Doumont was picked up as he strolled along the Promenade des Anglais in Nice without a care in the world, sampling the late autumnal afterglow of the world's playground after changing a thousand pounds sterling into francs, thinking in lustful anticipation of the bosomy night-club singer he was taking out to dinner that evening. He was stunned with disbelief when he was whisked into the police station and questioned none too gently about the murdered man who'd been found locked in his flat in Paris.

When detectives searched Alain's luggage at his hotel and found more than eighty thousand pounds in English currency, they made a brilliant wrong deduction about the crime: Alain Doumont had robbed the English bank robber, had lured him to his flat and killed him for his money. All the circumstantial evidence confirmed it and now the wretched Alain Doumont found himself the victim of Fate's most diabolocal frame-up.

The concierge in the old apartment house stubbornly maintained that she'd seen Doumont running away from his flat with his two suitcases as if the Devil was after him, and she'd never seen him since. She'd completely forgotten about the other man, similar in appearance to Alain, who'd arrived some time afterwards and gone upstairs never to come down. Or if she remembered she didn't think it worth mentioning. Another contributory factor to Doumont's guilt was the hasty letter of resignation he'd written to the Editor of *Le Figaro* on the day he disappeared, so that nobody would go to his flat looking for him and the body of his victim would not be found until his lease expired in four years' time.

The real assassin René Bruard was not likely to come forward and admit to shooting the wrong man in the

Rue Tournefort. Yvonne Belmondo had returned to England and could not be found to verify Alain's desperate insistence that it was she who had stolen the money from Blackstock and then hidden it in her lover's flat. Even if she had been questioned, Yvonne in her vindictive hatred would have been most likely to gloat over Alain's richly deserved fate. She would have left him to rot in the trap of his own devising.

The detectives practically laughed in Alain's face at the sottish naïveté of his desperate lying and wriggling. How could he rebut all the deadly incontrovertible facts that established his guilt? Who else could have shot the Englishman but the man who'd lured him to his flat in the Rue Tournefort, stolen his money and then decamped for the Cote d'Azur to spend it?

Alain Doumont came in for a further merciless grilling about what he'd done with the other half of the money when Robbery Squad detectives from Scotland Yard arrived at the Quai Des Orfèvres to repossess the stolen money found in Alain's possession. There was just over eighty thousand pounds in the white suitcase, but the English detectives insisted there should be double that amount from the two hundred thousand stolen in Dulwich. They weren't to know that the other half had been changed into Swiss francs and deposited in Joe Blackstock's numbered account.

As in the animal jungle all living things finally return their bodies to the ants, so in the financial jungle all illicit wealth in Swiss numbered accounts finally returns to the insatiable and imperishable Gnomes.

THE END

A LANCE FOR THE DEVIL
Robert Charles

The funeral service of Pope Paul VI was to be held in the great plaza before St. Peter's Cathedral in Rome, and was to be the scene of the most monstrous mass assassination of political leaders the world had ever known. Only Counter-Terror could prevent it.

IN THAT RICH EARTH
Alan Sewart

How long does it take for a human body to decay until only the bones remain? When Detective Sergeant Harry Chamberlane received news of a body, he raised exactly that question. But whose was the body? Who was to blame for the death and in what circumstances?

MURDER AS USUAL
Hugh Pentecost

A psychotic girl shot and killed Mac Crenshaw, who had come to the New England town with the advance party for Senator Farraday. Private detective David Cotter agreed that the girl was probably just a pawn in a complex game — but who had sent her on the assignment?

THE MARGIN
Ian Stuart

It is rumoured that Walkers Brewery has been selling arms to the South African army, and Graham Lorimer is asked to investigate. He meets the beautiful Shelley van Rynveld, who is dedicated to ending apartheid. When a Walkers employee is killed in a hit-and-run accident, his wife tells Graham that he's been seeing Shelly van Rynveld . . .

TOO LATE FOR THE FUNERAL
Roger Ormerod

Carol Turner, seventeen, and a mystery, is very close to a murder, and she has in her possession a weapon that could prove a number of things. But it is Elsa Mallin who suffers most before the truth of Carol Turner releases her.

NIGHT OF THE FAIR
Jay Baker

The gun was the last of the things for which Harry Judd had fought and now it was in the hands of his worst enemy, aimed at the boy he had tried to help. This was the night in which the past had to be faced again and finally understood.

MR CRUMBLESTONE'S EDEN

Henry Crumblestone was a quiet little man who would never knowingly have harmed another, and it was a dreadful twist of irony that caused him to kill in defence of a dream . . .

PAY-OFF IN SWITZERLAND
Bill Knox

'Hot' British currency was being smuggled to Switzerland to be laundered, hidden in a safari-style convoy heading across Europe. Jonathan Gaunt, external auditor for the Queen's and Lord Treasurer's Remembrancer, went along with the safari, posing as a tourist, to get any lead he could. But sudden death trailed the convoy every kilometer to Lake Geneva.

SALVAGE JOB
Bill Knox

A storm has left the oil tanker S.S. *Craig Michael* stranded and almost blocking the only channel to the bay at Cabo Esco. Sent to investigate, marine insurance inspector Laird discovers that the Portuguese bay is hiding a powder keg of international proportions.

BOMB SCARE — FLIGHT 147
Peter Chambers

Smog delayed Flight 147, and so prevented a bomb exploding in mid-air. Walter Keane found that during the crisis he had been robbed of his jewel bag, and Mark Preston was hired to locate it without involving the police. When a murder was committed, Preston knew the stake had grown.

STAMBOUL INTRIGUE
Robert Charles

Greece and Turkey were on the brink of war, and the conflict could spell the beginning of the end for the Western defence pact of N.A.T.O. When the rumour of a plot to speed this possibility reached Counter-espionage in Whitehall, Simon Larren and Adrian Cleyton were despatched to Turkey . . .

CRACK IN THE SIDEWALK
Basil Copper

After brilliant scientist Professor Hopcroft is knocked down and killed by a car, L.A. private investigator Mike Faraday discovers that his death was murder and that differing groups are engaged in a power struggle for The Zetland Method. As Mike tries to discover what The Zetland Method is, corpses and hair-breadth escapes come thick and fast . . .

DEATH OF A MACHINE
Charles Leader

When Mike M'Call found the mutilated corpse of a marine in an alleyway in Singapore, a thousand-strong marine battalion was hell-bent on revenge for their murdered comrade — and the next target for the tong gang of paid killers appeared to be M'Call himself . . .

ANYONE CAN MURDER
Freda Bream
Hubert Carson, the editorial Manager of the Herald Newspaper in Auckland, is found dead in his office. Carson's fellow employees knew that the unpopular chief reporter, Clive Yarwood, wanted Carson's job — but did he want it badly enough to kill for it?

CART BEFORE THE HEARSE
Roger Ormerod
Sometimes a case comes up backwards. When Ernest Connelly said 'I have killed . . . ', he did not name the victim. So Dave Mallin and George Coe find themselves attempting to discover a body to fit the crime.

SALESMAN OF DEATH
Charles Leader
For Mike M'Call, selling guns in Detroit proves a dangerous business — from the moment of his arrival in the middle of a racial plot, to the final clash of arms between two rival groups of militant extremists.

THE FOURTH SHADOW
Robert Charles

Simon Larren merely had to ensure that the visiting President of Maraquilla remained alive during a goodwill tour of the British Crown Colony of San Quito. But there were complications. Finally, there was a Communist-inspired bid for illegal independence from British rule, backed by the evil of voodoo.

SCAVENGERS AT WAR
Charles Leader

Colonel Piet Van Velsen needed an experienced officer for his mercenary commando, and Mike M'Call became a reluctant soldier. The Latin American Republic was torn apart by revolutionary guerrilla groups — but why were the ruthless Congo veterans unleashed on a province where no guerrilla threat existed?

MENACES, MENACES
Michael Underwood

Herbert Sipson, professional black-mailer, was charged with demanding money from a bingo company. Then, a demand from the Swallow Sugar Corporation also bore all the hallmarks of a Sipson scheme. But it arrived on the opening day of Herbert's Old Bailey trial — so how could he have been responsible?

MURDER WITH MALICE
Nicholas Blake

At the Wonderland holiday camp, someone calling himself The Mad Hatter is carrying out strange practical jokes that are turning increasingly malicious. Private Investigator Nigel Strangeways follows the Mad Hatter's trail and finally manages to make sense of the mayhem.

THE LONG NIGHT
Hartley Howard

Glenn Bowman is awakened by the 'phone ringing in the early hours of the morning and a woman he does not know invites him over to her apartment. When she tells him she wishes she was dead, he decides he ought to go and talk to her. It is a decision he is to bitterly regret when he finds himself involved in a case of murder . . .

THE LONELY PLACE
Basil Copper

The laconic L.A. private investigator Mike Faraday is hired to discover who is behind the death-threats to millionaire ex-silent movie star Francis Bolivar. Faraday finds a strange state of affairs at Bolivar's Gothic mansion, leading to a horrifying mass slaughter when a chauffeur goes berserk.

THE DARK MIRROR
Basil Copper

Californian private eye Mike Faraday reckons the case is routine, until a silenced gun cuts down Horvis the antique dealer and involves Mike in a trail of violence and murder.

DEADLY NIGHTCAP
Harry Carmichael

Mrs. Esther Payne was a very unpopular lady — right up to the night when she took two sleeping tablets and died. Traces of strychnine were discovered in the tube of pills, but only four people had the opportunity to obtain the poison for Esther's deadly night-cap . . .

DARK DESIGN
Freda Hurt

Caroline Lane missed her husband when he was away on his frequent business trips — until the mysterious phone-call that introduced Neil Fuller into her life. Then came doubts that led her to question her husband's real whereabouts, even his identity.

ESCAPE A KILLER
Judson Philips

Blinded by an acid-throwing fanatic, famous newspaperman Max Richmond moved to an isolated mansion in Connecticut. On a visit there, Peter Styles, a writer for NEWSVIEW MAGAZINE, became involved in a diabolical plot. The trap was not meant for him, but he was as helpless as the intended victim.

LONG RANGE DESERTER
David Bingley

Jack Walmer deserts from the French Foreign Legion to fight with a British Unit. Time and again, Jack must prove his allegiance by risking his life to save British servicemen. His final task is an attack on an Italian fortress, where the identity of a British prisoner holds the key to his future happiness.